MIXED UP

LOOK FOR MORE ACTION AND HUMOR FROM
GORDON KORMAN

The Fort

Linked

War Stories

Restart

Whatshisface

Slacker

Level 13

Radio Fifth Grade

The Toilet Paper Tigers

The Chicken Doesn't Skate

This Can't Be Happening at Macdonald Hall!

THE SWINDLE SERIES

Swindle
Zoobreak
Framed
Showoff
Hideout
Jackpot
Unleashed
Jingle

The Hypnotists series

The Titanic trilogy

The Kidnapped trilogy

The On the Run series

The Dive trilogy

The Everest trilogy

The Island trilogy

MIXED UP

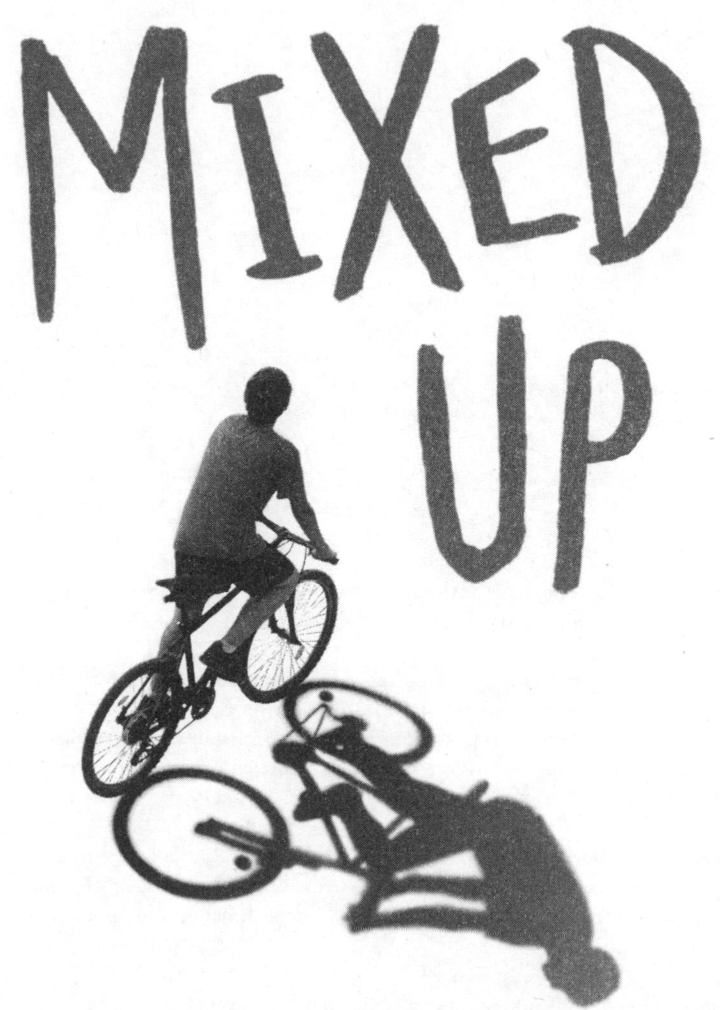

GORDON KORMAN

SCHOLASTIC PRESS / NEW YORK

Library of Congress Cataloging-in-Publication Data available

ISBN 978-1-338-82672-2

10 9 8 7 6 5 4 3 2 1 23 24 25 26 27

Printed in Italy 183
First edition, July 2023

Book design by Elizabeth B. Parisi

FOR RAYMOND JARDINE (@THEAMELPOS)

MIXED UP

CHAPTER ONE

REEF MOODY

The instant Willis calls "Dinner!" the stampede is on.

Liam hip-checks me aside as I make for the stairs. He's a high school senior—a football player—and outweighs me by a hundred pounds. Carolyn, 16, blows past me on the landing, planting an elbow in my sternum that plainly says: *Me first.*

I could probably catch up, but I'm not really hungry anyway and it isn't worth the fight.

Fact is, I haven't been hungry in almost a year.

By the time I make it to the kitchen, Declan, 14, is at the counter, loading up a plate while holding the other two back with a well-placed shoulder. While he's the youngest of the Helmer siblings, he's still got two years on me. Liam and Carolyn aren't too bad. They ignore me, but at least it's okay with them that I'm alive. Not Declan. Declan hates my guts. I'm not his brother. I'm not related to anybody in the Helmer house.

I'm the charity case.

By the time I make it to the hot plate, there's only one piece of chicken left—the one nobody wanted. It's small, dried out, and burnt at the edges. If I could, I'd give it back its feathers and send it on its way.

With a sigh, I scoop it onto my plate, add some rice and carrots, and head for the table. Like I said, I'm not hungry, but I know I might as well eat. If I don't, Willis and Jenna will ask questions. Jenna was Mom's best friend, and she worries about me. That's why I live with the Helmers.

Live—I hate using that word. I prefer to think of myself as a very long-term houseguest who's going to move out of here and go someplace else—*any*place else—as soon as I can. And however much I want that, multiply it by a thousand and you've got Declan. Here he was, the baby of the family, and along comes some poor orphan who's two years younger, with a sob story that would melt an iceberg. Presto, he has to share his room with the interloper.

Lost in my melancholy thoughts, I don't see the elbow come shooting out at me. With deadly accuracy, Declan delivers just the right amount of bump to the bottom of my dish. It isn't enough force to make me drop the plate, but carrots go flying, rice sprays against the wall like it's coming from a hose, and that dried-up little chicken cutlet hits the dining room carpet and sticks there in a stain of sauce.

Liam is a no-nonsense eater. He doesn't even look up. Carolyn laughs out loud and mutters, "Walk much, or just read about it?"

"Yeah, you clumsy oaf!" Declan chimes in. "Watch where you're going. That's *our* carpet you just ruined!"

Declan is always quick to talk about what's "ours," his real point being that it's not mine.

Never mind that the dining room carpet had plenty of stains to begin with before I got here, and that even brand-new, it was never the million-dollar Persian rug in the main reception room of Buckingham Palace. He gets just as possessive over "our" Tic Tacs and "our" toilet paper.

Jenna and I bump heads in our effort to clean up the mess.

"Sorry," I mumble, even though I have nothing to apologize for. That's another thing about being the charity case: Everything feels like it's your fault, even when it isn't. Just being there is offense enough. Besides, nobody saw Declan's elbow. He has a knack for that.

Jenna sighs, but her words are delivered in a light, friendly tone. "Reef, what are we going to do with you?"

"Maybe I should practice walking with a book balanced on my head," I offer in a pretty pathetic attempt at humor.

Actually, the pathetic part is that I don't even try to tell Jenna and Willis what really happened—and that their darling son is a giant jerk. Why would I say something like that to the only people nice enough to take me in when Mom died? And, more to the point, why would they believe me? Declan's their kid and I'm not.

"Tell you what," Willis suggests in an attempt to sound cheerful. "I'll scramble you a couple of eggs."

"That's fine. I'm okay with this," I reply, picking a tuft of carpet fuzz off the chicken.

Meanwhile, Declan is stuffing his face like all this has nothing to do with him.

Eventually, I'm alone in the kitchen, gagging down scrambled eggs on toast, Willis's specialty. Ketchup makes it more bearable, but only a little. I hate feeling sorry for myself, especially since everybody else already feels sorry for me. Except Declan, of course. He wants me dead.

Dead. I drop my fork with a clatter. I've promised myself never to use that word in a joking way. Not now that Mom is dead for real.

Dead is no joke. It's permanent and final. Who knows that better than me?

At that awful thought, a mouthful of eggs and toast is just about reaching the point of no return in my throat. I want to spit it out, but after the mess in the dining room, I don't dare decorate the kitchen too. And I know I have to eat. Eating isn't a problem anywhere else. Just in this house.

I work up a Herculean swallow and choke it down. It scratches all the way to my stomach, where it sits like a bowling ball.

Don't barf, I command myself. *It'll make Declan too happy.*

The last time I saw my mother was on my phone. The nurse FaceTimed me so I could say goodbye. Mom was on a ventilator, so she couldn't talk to me. I remember all the tubes and monitors surrounding her. Her skin reminded me of the pages of really old books—yellowed and paper thin. The intensive care ward was crowded with doctors and nurses, each one wrapped in layers of protective gear. You could barely hear their muffled voices over the clicking, sucking, and beeping of the machines.

Violently, I shake my head to force the horrible picture away. It visits me every single night, so I refuse to put up with it during the day, when I'm in control of what I think about. Anyway, the worst part isn't that image or any image. It's the fact that what happened to Mom was my fault.

I turn it over in my head again and again, although all it ever does is make me feel even more miserable. I'm wracking my brain for that one crossroads, that instant in time when something could have gone a little differently and I wouldn't be living with the Helmers because Mom would still be here. I'm not sure what I think I'm "searching" for—I can already pinpoint the exact second that set this tragedy in motion. It was the moment Portia Banyon invited me to her birthday party.

No—that makes it sound like I'm blaming Portia. It wasn't the invitation. It was the fact that I talked Mom into letting me go.

The pandemic finally seemed like it was going to end. We thought Covid was almost over. Stores and restaurants were open. People were doing things again—going to movies, hosting get-togethers, shaking hands.

And yet Mom was really torn about me going to that party. She kept talking about how the virus was still out there. "In a few more months, everything will be back to normal," she told me again and again. "Then you can go to all the parties you want."

But I didn't want to go to all the parties; I wanted to go to this one. Portia was the most popular girl in our neighborhood.

Being invited was a big deal. It meant she knew I existed. And in spite of the fact that we'd been in classes together on and off since forever, this hadn't always been the case.

At last Mom gave in, even though it was obvious that she didn't want to. Guess I just wore her down. You get good at that when you're an only child.

Two days after the party, Portia wasn't in school. They said she had a fever of 103. The next day: me too. That afternoon Mom came home from work early. At first, I thought it was to take care of me.

It was to take care of herself.

We had all the classic symptoms—fever, cough, then a loss of taste and smell. A candy bar might as well have been a cake of soap. We took Covid tests, and the results were positive. Breakthrough cases for both of us.

We went home from the clinic to hunker down until we got better. I did. She didn't.

A week later, she checked herself into the hospital and I went to stay with the Helmers until my mother came home again.

She never did.

I always do my homework on my stomach on the living room floor. There's a desk in the room I share with Declan. But I spend as little time up there as possible, because there's also Declan.

I can't put it off forever, though. Eventually, I have to go to sleep, and the living room floor isn't an option for that, as much as I'd prefer it.

Declan is on his bed, listening to music on his phone. In his hands, he's turning over a roundish geode, with dramatic purple amethyst crystals on the inside.

"Mr. DeVine has one a lot like that," I comment. Mr. DeVine is our school librarian. He found his geode while rock climbing on the Canadian Shield. It's his pride and joy.

I'm honestly just making conversation. Sometimes I try to talk to Declan like we're two normal humans. That shows how delusional I am.

"There's more than one rock in the world, Reek!" Declan snaps angrily. "This one's mine." *Reek* is his nickname for me, which is unfair, since he's the one who's a big stinker.

That's when it dawns on me: Declan's geode and Mr. DeVine's are the same geode. I should have known. Declan is a master of the five-finger discount. His room—our room—is piled high with stuff that other people are still looking for. Liam and Carolyn know what he's like, but Willis and Jenna have no clue. Why do the parents of the worst kids always think they're angels?

I can't resist. "Why, because you picked it up and walked out of the library?"

It happens in a split second. With wrist action alone, Declan chucks Mr. DeVine's geode at my head. I feel the wind as it zooms past my ear, missing me by about an eighth of an inch. It hits the far wall with a *crack* and splits in two.

"What's that racket?" Willis demands from downstairs.

"Sorry!" I call back, even though I was the target. We charity cases are always quick to apologize. The urge is uncontrollable, a survival instinct. Or maybe for me it's because, no matter how innocent I am, deep down I know I'm guilty of something much worse.

To Declan, I say, "Now you can't even bring it back, because it's broken."

With a snort, he rolls over, and the geode and I are officially gone from his mind. Classic Declan. He didn't even want Mr. DeVine's pride and joy from the Canadian Shield. He took it because it was there.

In our room, the war is already over. That's a rare good thing about Declan: He can come down from a rage just as fast as he goes up into one.

He's also the kind of person who falls asleep the instant his head hits the pillow. That's what you get from having a clear conscience—ha ha. Maybe I'm just jealous, because I lie awake half the night, sifting through old memories. You do a lot of remembering when memories are all you've got.

I think about Portia's party a ton. It was decently fun, although nothing could ever have been as good as I was expecting it to be. Mostly, I just loved being there with the cool people. Nowadays, I replay it in my mind, searching for the stray cough or the fever-flushed face that supplied the virus I brought home to Mom. Or maybe it was Portia herself. She got sick before I did. I'll probably never know, and it wouldn't make any difference if I did. Mom will still be gone.

But I can't help myself. As I get a little drowsier, the memories march on. Mom serving me breakfast—I've always hated oatmeal. The two of us shopping for school clothes, me trying to drag her away from the sale rack. Working in the garden, sprinkling fertilizer around the tomato plants—

I sit bolt upright in confusion. Tomato plants? What tomato plants?

We lived in an apartment. There was no vegetable garden. How can I be remembering something that never happened?

Could this have been at a friend's house, where I helped out with some gardening? A school field trip to a farm somewhere?

No, I've never fertilized plants before. I'd bet anything on that. I don't even know what fertilizer is supposed to look like. This stuff could be kitty litter, for all I can tell the difference.

And yet I *do* know. It's part of the memory. Also that these tomatoes are called Roma and they're grown mostly for spaghetti sauce. I think harder, focusing on the recollection, waiting for the "oh yeah" moment that will explain where all this comes from. There are other plants next to tomatoes—green beans, as a matter of fact. They're not as healthy as they should be. Again, I have no idea why *that* thought would come from me.

Across the room, Declan shifts on his pillow with a loud, juicy snore. The garden memory fades.

I lie back down. All that must have come from somewhere, but I'm too tired to figure it out now. And really, who cares?

When your whole life has fallen apart, the last thing you want to stress over is Roma tomatoes.

CHAPTER TWO

THEO METZINGER

I see the teeth first, with the sunlight gleaming off of them. I can't believe how big they are.

Jaws. The name comes to me straight from the movie that fueled most of my nightmares when I was younger. But the teeth from the film were part of a twenty-five-foot-long killer shark. And these are attached to . . . a *rabbit*!

He's poised at the foot of the maple tree, utterly frozen, like he thinks I can't see him. In reality, the opposite is true. He's *all* I can see—his teeth, anyway. The two front ones are the size of postage stamps. Okay, that's not exactly great-white territory, but on a two-pound rabbit, they draw the eye—especially when they're aimed in the direction of the flower bed by the garage.

When he bursts into action, it's like he's been shot out of a cannon. I burst into action too. As I race toward him, I pull the yellow belt from my karate gi and snap it in his direction.

He veers off from the pansies and makes an end run for the marigolds at the far end of the flower bed. But I'm onto him, waving the belt like a whip.

"Get out of here! Beat it!"

My father appears at the gate. "What are you doing, Theo? We're late for karate!"

"I can't let Jaws eat my flowers!" I shout back.

"Jaws?"

"The rabbit!"

"I don't see any rabbit. Get in the car."

"But he's the one!" I accuse him in outrage. "Something's been nibbling at all the new shoots and blossoms for weeks! It's him!"

It's not the explanation my father wants to hear. "Fix your gi and into the car. Now!"

As I retie my yellow belt, I notice that one of the ends has black earth on it. I hope Dad doesn't see.

The Seidokwan dojo where I take karate isn't very far away. I could totally walk. Dad only drives me to make sure I go.

I don't hate the karate part, although I don't love it much either. My complaint is the reason my parents signed me up in the first place. It's because I need to "toughen up"—Dad's words, not mine.

My father is a big guy, so when he drives, he's not so much *at* the wheel as *over* it, peering through the windshield as if looking for targets to shoot at with his lasers. "What was that song and dance with the rabbit? He's not bothering you—why do you have to bother him?"

"He *is* bothering me," I insist. "He's destroying my plants."

Dad snorts. "Yeah, well, maybe we should give him a medal. What twelve-year-old kid gives a hoot about *plants*? There's a whole wide world out there, Theo! You've got to reach out and grab it by the throat! When I was your age, there was no stopping me! I ruled the school!"

My father talks about that a lot. I guess he was kind of a ringleader when he was a kid. A sports star, a troublemaker, a bro . . . but not the kind who gets suspended; the kind everybody secretly admires. I don't think he has anything against flowers and vegetables. It just bugs him that gardening is what I do instead of being more like him.

I try to reason with him. "I'm not you, Dad. I'm me."

"You don't have to be *me*. I know it sounds like I'm dumping all over your hobby, but one day you're going to thank me for being hard on you."

That might be true. But that one day is not today. The whole hour I'm at the dojo, getting punched and kicked and rolling around the mat, all I can think of is Jaws sinking those big buckteeth into my flowers.

"How was your workout?" Dad asks when he picks me up after class.

"Okay." That's been my standard answer ever since I started martial arts.

Dad points to a group of boys and girls heading into the 7-Eleven down the block. "Aren't those kids from karate?"

I can't resist. "No, they're just regular people who like to walk around in karate suits instead of normal clothes."

"All right, smart guy. Why aren't you with them?"

"Because they're total strangers?"

He slaps the steering wheel in exasperation. "This is what you turn into when you hang around snap peas instead of people! They're not strangers—you're in class with them twice a week. In my day, I'd be the leader of the pack in the first five minutes. And you're too shy to say, 'Yeah, I'm coming with you guys.'"

"Nobody invited me," I point out.

"Who waits to be invited? You just go." He throws the car in gear, pulls up beside the group filing into the 7-Eleven, and blasts the horn.

They turn around and look at us, confused and irritated. I slump down into my seat. I swear, if I could fit into the glove compartment, I'd be in there.

My dojo-mates disappear into the store.

Dad looks at me and shakes his head. "You blew it."

"Can we go home now?"

When we get back to the house, I race to the flower bed. Jaws couldn't have been that hungry, because the pansies are only damaged around the edges. But the marigolds must have been extra delicious. The blooms are gone, leaving nothing but empty stems. I scan the yard. No sign of the rabbit. I hope he's doubled over in a hedge somewhere, suffering from a killer stomachache.

I check the vegetable garden out back, almost afraid to look. So far everything is untouched. Jaws hasn't found it yet. But that won't last forever.

Inside the house, my nine-year-old sister is telling Dad about her soccer game, and he's lapping it up.

"Guess what, Theo," he calls to me. "Kristi scored two goals today!"

"No way. That's great, kid." I try to sound like I mean it. It isn't Kristi's fault that she's the son my father never had. Well, not really, but she's his best chance at a child who rules the school. She already rules our house.

I head up to my room to change out of the gi. My eyes are immediately drawn to the notebook on my nightstand. I've been making an effort to remember my dreams. They're always vivid in my mind in the middle of the night—but by the time I wake up in the morning, I've totally forgotten them.

That's what the notebook is for. Mid-dream, I slap myself awake enough to scribble down the details. It's a surefire way to ruin a good dream, and a lot of my notes are barely readable, and pretty weird besides. But it's really important that I keep doing this.

Lately, I've been remembering things that never happened in my life. The only possible explanation is that I'm dreaming them, and then remembering my dreams like they were real. But I'll never be able to prove that if my dreams are gone as soon as I dream them.

I flip through the notebook, wishing I'd worked a little harder back in third grade when Ms. Fitzpatrick taught us handwriting. I can barely read my own words. In all fairness, though, when you wake up screaming from a terrifying nightmare, the least of your worries is *neatness counts*.

I peer at the scribbles. *Park slide turns into giant boa.* I'm pretty sure I meant a boa constrictor, not the big fluffy feather boas old movie stars wore around their necks.

Can't open my locker and the lock is heating up and burning my fingers. That must have been one of my frustration dreams, where I'm trying to do something or get someplace and I just can't make it happen. I have a lot of those—like I'm walking to school and the building keeps moving farther away, or I'm climbing stairs but I never get to the top.

Grizzly bear wearing dad's high school football jersey. Kind of a tight squeeze, but to be fair, it doesn't really fit Dad anymore either.

I slam the notebook back onto the nightstand. Burning locks, giant snakes, grizzlies—none of this explains the memories I've been experiencing. Those memories are almost . . . normal. Or at least they would be if they were things that had actually happened to me. And I'm ninety-nine percent sure they never did.

Here's an example: I'm at school, but the floor tiles are *wrong.* I mean, they're real tiles, just not the ones my school actually has. And as I leave for the day, I pass by the main office on the way out the door. Except that's not where the office is supposed to be. It should be farther back, next to the cafeteria.

Outside isn't right either. The front walk is brickwork instead of large concrete slabs. Since when? And why is the parking lot off to the left? That's when I turn back in the direction of the building and the explanation becomes clear. My middle school is a sprawling structure with a flat roof, kind of squarish, with big windows and a lot of metal. This one looks nothing like that. It's old style, with dark red brick, three stories, and a large, white-painted cupola on the roof.

In other words . . . it isn't my school. I've never laid eyes on this place in my life. So why do I remember being there?

There's a knock on my door and Mom steps into the bedroom.

"What?" I ask. It comes out a little sharper than I intended it. Poor Mom usually ends up the peacemaker between my father and me. It can't be fun for her to be caught in the middle like that.

"I understand you and Dad got into it a little after karate."

I shrug. "Sue me, I'm not the rule-the-school type."

"He loved middle school," she tries to explain. "And he wants that for you too."

I wonder which middle school I'm supposed to love—the one I go to or the one in my weird memories?

She walks over to the nightstand and picks up the notebook. "Are you keeping a diary?"

"Not exactly," I mumble, then add anxiously, "Don't read it!"

She flushes. "Actually, I did glance through it a couple of days ago. I didn't really understand much of it. What is it—ideas for stories?"

Uh-oh, now I'm in it. How am I ever going to explain the boa constrictor or the bear in Dad's football shirt?

So I tell her about writing down my dreams to see if they're the source of my strange memories.

She tries to be sympathetic. "Sometimes, when things are stressful, the mind can—"

"I'm not stressed, Mom," I interrupt. "I'm just remembering stuff I shouldn't remember."

Now she looks alarmed. "Exactly what kind of memories are we talking about?"

"Real ones. With bricks and parking lots and cupolas."

Through the window, a blur of gray-brown fur catches my attention. It's Jaws in the backyard—which means the vegetables are in danger.

I sprint out the door.

"Where are you going?" Mom demands. "You can't tell me something like this and just run away."

"Sorry—this is an emergency!"

I fly down the stairs, my one goal to protect my garden from the puffy-tailed menace.

There's nothing wrong with my memory of Jaws.

CHAPTER THREE

REEF MOODY

When your life comes crashing down around your ears, everyone else's life just goes on like things are normal. Because, for them, things are.

The kickball game at recess, for instance.

That game used to be a big part of my life. I was second in home runs behind Kendrick Rizzo, who almost doesn't count, because he wore size thirteen shoes in the sixth grade. I used to spend every morning looking forward to lunch, and every afternoon reliving the game in my mind. All the other players—boys and girls—were my friends. I'll bet sixty percent of the conversations I had at Delgado Middle School were about kickball. And it would have been closer to a hundred percent if we didn't have classes and homework and stuff like that.

Now? I don't even leave the lunchroom unless they boot me out to get some fresh air. The excited shouts and cheering from the diamond mean nothing to me. When a gigantic home run sails deep into the outfield, I don't even glance over to see who kicked it. Fact is, that's just not my world anymore. I don't know what is, but it definitely isn't kickball.

I once overheard Jenna describing me to Willis as "lost." That isn't right either. I'm not lost. It's more like, when something really, *really* bad happens, you stop caring. About everything. I don't have friends anymore. They're still around, giving me space, waiting for me to be ready to come to them. But I'm not sure if it's ever going to happen. It's been almost a year since Mom died, and when you stay away from people that long, you sort of become strangers again.

Don't get me wrong. I'm not mad at anybody. I don't expect the kickball players to shut down their game forever because I had a death in the family. That's the upside of not caring: Nothing bothers you that much, because the very worst thing has happened already.

When the bell rings, I usually try to get out of the cafeteria before the kickball players come back inside, but today I'm running late. Ms. Wallace sent me to the nurse because I dozed off in her class. Declan has been tossing peanuts at me in the middle of the night lately. They don't hurt that much, but you get so uptight waiting for the next one that it becomes impossible to fall asleep. So I'm still working on my sandwich when the teams come clattering in the way I used to—happy, laughing, and talking a mile a minute.

I turn away from the open door, but it's already too late. There's Portia, rosy-cheeked, breathless, and smiling. She's the one I can't look at and she's also the one I can't look away from. She's walking with some new girl, and as they pass by, I hear her whisper, "His mom died last year. Covid."

Not a single word of that is wrong. But hearing it from her makes the hair on the back of my neck stand up straight.

Last year, the school district made me see a special counselor, because they were afraid I might have a breakdown. I didn't—not back then. But now I'm starting to wonder if it's happening to me in small ways.

For example, I've been remembering the school wrong. Yesterday, I went to the drinking fountain and it was in the wrong place. It was supposed to be in the middle of the hall, but it was all the way down at the end. Not only that, but I stood back because it shoots really high. So how come it was barely dribbling?

Went around to a couple of other fountains, and they barely dribbled too. Why do I remember getting a geyser in the face?

It's like how I remembered gardening when I know for a fact that I've never planted anything in my life. How can you remember things that didn't happen unless you're losing it?

Which brings me to the rabbit. He's brown and furry, with two big square front teeth. And sure, I've seen rabbits before. There are wild ones all around town. But for some reason, this rabbit scares me. Who's afraid of a rabbit? Rabbits are afraid of everything, and I'm afraid of this one? How is that possible?

I do not know this rabbit, yet somehow I remember him. I even know his name: *Jaws.*

I may be losing my mind, but at least I have a sense of humor.

It makes no sense, because I'm positive I could never be afraid of a rabbit, or any small, harmless animal like that. Animals like me. Mom and I had dozens of pets—hamsters, lizards, gerbils, turtles, guinea pigs. We're animal people. I catch myself—we *were* animal people. I still have trouble getting used to thinking of my mother in the past tense.

I picture her cradling Vanilla, our hamster. There's Vanilla's little pink snout and beady eyes. But when I try to remember Mom . . . she's kind of indistinct. I *see* her—but not in any detail. What happened to the brilliant green eyes, the smile she couldn't hide when she was holding one of our pets?

Her face is just a blur.

Panic rises up my spine, and I have to hold myself back from screaming. Am I *forgetting* my mother? Frantically, I slap myself in the head, the way you whack a vending machine that didn't give you your candy bar.

A couple of eighth-grade girls shoot me a strange look as they pass in the hallway. I guess it's not every day you see a guy beating the snot out of himself.

I whip out my phone and swipe madly through the photographs. It's a huge relief that I have so many shots of Mom. It was just the two of us as far back as I can remember. I never knew my father. According to Mom, he was out of the picture before I was born. Jenna mentioned something about trying to get in touch with him after my mother died, but nobody could find him, and I'm okay with that. My family was always just Mom and me.

And now it's just me.

I scroll from photo to photo, drinking in Mom's features. But when I try to call up her image in my mind, I get the same blur. And when I force-fill in the details, I'm not remembering Mom; I'm remembering the face from the pictures on my phone . . . which isn't exactly the same thing.

What kind of monster forgets his poor dead mother? Especially when I'm the one who—

No. Don't go there. I know all too well what I did.

"Reef Moody!"

Uh-oh. Principal Latimore is bearing down on me, her impossibly high heels clicking on the floor. "You know the rule about phone use during school hours."

"I wasn't using it. I was just—" What was I doing? Reminding myself what my own mother looked like? I'd rather be sent to Alcatraz than admit that.

"Give it to me, please." She holds out a manicured hand.

I hesitate. You know how people sometimes say, "My whole life is on that phone"? Well, in my case, that's actually true. If I lose these pictures, I'm left with the blur.

On the other hand, it's not like I'm losing my phone forever. I'll get it back at three thirty. But what if it gets lost? Or dropped? Or handed back to the wrong person? I can't take that chance. Those pictures are all I have left—especially now that I can't even trust my own memory!

I judge the distance down the hall to the main exit. I can make it. There's no way Latimore can catch me on those high heels. Sure, I'll be in twice as much trouble when I come back, but at least I won't have to give up my phone.

I'm poised for flight. But as she reaches for the device, she catches sight of the picture on the display: Mom at the beach with me, age seven.

The principal's face softens, and for an instant, she looks like she only wants to expel two or three students instead of the usual five hundred. She withdraws her painted fingernails. "Put your phone away, Reef. And remember to keep it off during school hours."

She clicks away, never knowing how close she came to a prison break.

The Helmers live on a dead-end street a few minutes' walk from Delgado. It's less than a mile from where I used to live with Mom, but it always feels alien, like I took a wrong turn and ended up in a strange neighborhood.

The house isn't exactly small, but it always feels slightly overcrowded. To be fair, Willis, Jenna, and their three kids fit perfectly. I'm the overcrowding. I guess nobody ever thinks they're going to have to force-adopt some poor orphan.

I pause before opening the front door. I hate this place, but I totally understand that what I really hate is the reason I have to live here. I know all too well where I'd be if Willis and Jenna hadn't taken me in: an institution or orphanage, somewhere with no connection to Mom at all. The Helmers are the nicest people in the world for saving me from all that—especially Jenna, for being Mom's best friend. And I do appreciate them—even if, most of the time, I'm too miserable to show it.

When I let myself in, I don't toss my backpack on the kitchen counter, like every other kid. That's something you do at home. Instead, I drag it upstairs to the room I share with Declan. That isn't home either, but it's the closest thing I have right now. I shove the bag under my bed, where Declan won't see it. I used to leave it leaning against the desk, but he filled it with Jell-O once. I don't make that mistake anymore.

My eyes are instantly drawn to the small framed photograph of Mom that I keep on my nightstand. I see it every day, but now it seems like the most important thing I own. If my phone had gotten confiscated, and somehow broken or lost, this would have been my only picture of my mother. For some reason, the fact that it didn't happen is no comfort. I sit down on the bed and cradle the plastic frame like it's delicate crystal.

Not sure how long I've been zoned out in that position when the book comes flying in at me. It knocks the picture out of my hands, sending it spiraling through the air. I can hear the glass break as it hits the wall.

Shocked, I look up. Declan is in the doorway, a laughing sneer on his smarmy face.

The next thing I know, I'm up on my feet, stalking toward him. As the room around me fades behind a red haze of rage, I throw myself at Declan. I'm not thinking about what I'm doing. It's pure gut reaction. As I bear down on him, my knee comes up toward my chest, and my leg snaps out, my foot catching him right below the jaw. The impact is so great that he lifts off the floor and lands flat on his back, several feet out into the hall.

He lies there, stunned, and I back away, my thoughts whirling. *Why did I do that? This kid belongs here and I don't! If I get myself kicked out of the Helmer house, what then?*

Declan gets to his feet, which is a good thing, I guess, because it means I didn't really hurt him. "You'll pay for that," he promises in a low voice.

I almost apologize. But then I look at Mom's picture, the jagged crack in the glass across her face. I stick out my chin and keep my mouth shut.

Declan holds his ground for a few seconds longer, staring at me through eyes that are barely slits. Then he turns his back and stomps downstairs.

I examine my picture. The glass is broken, the frame is cracked, but the photo is intact. I lie back on my bed, but my relief is short-lived. *You'll pay for that.* Declan's exact words. I have no doubt that he meant them one thousand percent. Declan Helmer probably delivers on every threat he makes. He's an eighth grader at my school, even though he's two years older than me and should be a freshman. Nobody talks about how or why that happened, but it's pretty obvious. Declan and trouble are old friends, and that includes the kind of trouble that involves the police. Mom used to talk about poor Jenna, who had so many problems with her younger son.

Which means I'd better grow eyes in the back of my head or some other early warning system for when Declan comes after me, because he will. The only thing slowing him down might be the fact that I was able to lay him out just now.

In spite of myself, I can't help feeling a twinge of satisfaction at the mental picture of my foot connecting with his jaw.

The happy moment passes quickly and I sit trembling on the edge of my bed. It was great to deck Declan, but how did I do it? That kick was something straight out of a martial arts movie.

I don't know martial arts.

I try to relive the moment. My knee rose up; my body balanced; my leg struck out. But I didn't make it happen; I wouldn't know how. It was more like my body did it without me. Like muscle memory, where you never forget how to ride a bike or swing a baseball bat.

Except that muscle memory only works when you knew how to do the thing in the first place.

What's happening to me?

CHAPTER FOUR

THEO METZINGER

Dr. Abagnale peers at me through her thick horn-rimmed glasses. "Tell me about the rabbit."

I sit up sharply and stare at the psychiatrist. The *rabbit*? That's what she got out of all this? Everything that's going on in my life, and she thinks the problem is the *rabbit*?

A piece of friendly advice: Don't try to write down your dreams. And if you do, make sure the notebook never falls into the hands of your parents. Mine did, and here I am, three days later, in a psychiatrist's office.

Dr. Abagnale is one of those *we* people. She always talks about *we* and *us*, when what she really means is me. Maybe she thinks this makes us a team—the two of us against the world, side by side, in this together.

"Sometimes," she continues, "we deal with the things we can't control by creating someone to blame—a monster, a stranger, an *animal*."

"The rabbit's *real*," I insist. "He's eating the flowers, and it's only a matter of time before he gets around to the vegetable garden."

"I know the rabbit is real to *you*—"

I cut her off. "He's real to everybody! He's a real rabbit! Dad knows!"

"Your father's the one who mentioned to me that you're the only one who sees that rabbit," Dr. Abagnale explains.

I gaze longingly at the office door, imagining myself making a break for freedom. That's what Jaws always does, but he doesn't have parents ready to ground him for taking off. Like it or not—and I don't—I'm stuck here with Dr. Abagnale.

"Look, I'm not afraid to admit that there's something screwy going on with me. But it's not about the rabbit. It's the fact that I'm remembering things I shouldn't be remembering, because they never happened. If you're going to concentrate on something, why not that?"

I already told Dr. Abagnale some of the memories I'm worried about. She doesn't seem to be worried too.

"You're twelve years old now, Theo. We have a lot of experience in our rearview mirror. Our brains can be like a computer hard drive that's running out of space. We can't add new memories without deleting some of the old files. Details get forgotten, mixed up. It's completely normal."

"What about that school with the white cupola on top?" I challenge. "I've only been to three different schools in my life. None of them had that."

She shrugs. "Perhaps you saw it once in a movie, or as an illustration in a book. Or it could be a symbol, like the rabbit."

"The rabbit is real," I manage through clenched teeth. "And so were the flowers he ate."

"Our minds constantly generate symbols," she goes on. "A cupola could represent tradition or authority. Or a distant goal that seems out of our reach . . ."

Even though I'm pretty sure she's wrong, I find myself actually trying to make myself agree with her. She's the one with the posh office and the fancy-looking diplomas all over the wall. She must be smart, right? Why am I worrying when an actual medical professional is telling me there's nothing to worry about?

And there on the psychiatrist's couch, I have the most frightening memory of all. I'm standing in the bushes outside a big building. It must be a hospital, because my face is pressed up against a window and I'm staring in at a hospital room. Doctors and nurses in face shields with layers of plastic over their clothes swarm around the patient in the bed. But here's the thing—I know her. I mean, I don't. But in the memory, she's someone close to me—close enough that seeing her so sick is tearing me apart.

"Theo?" the doctor prompts. "Are we listening?"

"Yeah, yeah. I'm good."

But I'm not good. Dr. Abagnale almost had me convinced that what's been happening to me is no big deal. What my mind just played for me was no symbol. It was a memory.

A memory of the worst day of somebody's life.

I see Dr. Abagnale on Mondays and Wednesdays. That leaves Tuesdays and Thursdays for karate class. I guess two is the magic number of times per week for my parents to force me to do something I hate.

By my third session, the psychiatrist says I'm making progress. In my opinion, the one making progress is Dr. Abagnale. She now accepts the fact that there really is a rabbit named Jaws. This breakthrough only happened because I showed her a video on my phone. The quality wasn't great, and Jaws was just a blur, but you could still see those gigantic white choppers in detail.

"Good nickname" was her only comment.

Since she's accepted that I'm not making up imaginary rabbits, Dr. Abagnale's new thing is my relationship with my father. She thinks I don't like my dad, which might be a little bit true. But even if it is, I tell her it's only because he doesn't seem to like me very much. I understand why. He was popular, and when I think of kids like that in my own school right now, they don't much like me either. Well, maybe that's a little too strong. The truth is probably closer to they don't know I exist. I'm not into sports; I'm not super social; and, let's face it, there aren't a ton of gardening fans like me in your average middle school. Sue me, I love the idea that you can stick tiny seeds in the ground, water them, and a few weeks later, you've got something out of nothing—something that can feed people or decorate a room. How cool is that? The only thing twelve-year-old Dad had to do with gardens was to raid them in the middle of the night when he needed tomatoes to throw at passing cars.

Dr. Abagnale is wide-eyed. "Tomatoes at cars? Are you sure?"

"Oh yeah. He brags about it. Middle school was the happiest time of his life."

"Well . . ." Her mind is working so furiously that I can almost hear the gears grinding. "Maybe the point is that he remembers childhood as a time of freedom and creativity and experimentation. We can't blame him for that."

"I'm not blaming him for anything," I reply honestly. "But I might as well be some space alien who dropped from Alpha Centauri. He'll never understand what makes me tick."

"Yet he's *trying*," she persists. "And that's the important thing."

Well, even if he's trying, he's definitely not trying super hard. He's twenty minutes late to pick me up. And when he does finally appear, he screeches around the corner and squeals to a halt in front of me, annoyed that I'm not getting in the car fast enough.

"Hurry!" he rasps.

When I get in, my butt hasn't even made contact with the leather when he stomps on the gas. Our acceleration shuts my door and pins me to the seat.

"What's the rush?" I complain.

The answer comes in sentence bursts as he weaves through the traffic, honking and cursing at the other drivers. "The Comets are down a goal! . . . I had to leave to get you! . . . If they lose, they're out of the playoffs!"

Now I get it. The Clayton Comets are the fourth-grade soccer team my sister, Kristi, is the star of—and the main focus of Dad's life these days. If I can't rule the school, Kristi has to.

"Could you drop me home before you go back to the game?" I ask. "I want to harvest the new batch of snap peas while the pods are still tender."

"No time! Sophie Breeger got a red card, so we're playing a man down—I mean, a girl. Our backs are against the wall!"

"How does a nine-year-old get herself kicked out of a soccer game?" I wonder aloud.

"Who cares? It happened—that's all that matters!" We swerve into the school parking lot and roar up to the athletic field.

By the time I get the door open, Dad is already clattering up the metal bleachers. I hesitate. I can totally walk home from here, but if I don't stay, I'm never going to hear the end of it. Plus I really do want to show support for my kid sister—although I suspect Dad cares about this game a lot more than Kristi does.

When I join my father in the stands, I can't help noticing that most of the sparse crowd isn't even watching the game. It's basically a handful of moms chatting with each other, reading magazines, or scrolling on their phones. If there's anything they're ignoring more than the action on the field, it's Dad, who cheers himself hoarse every time Kristi touches the ball.

"I don't know you," I tell him as I sit down a good distance away.

"Cro-o-oss!" he brays at the top of his lungs.

And if you think he's worked up now, you should see him when Kristi scores the tying goal with eighteen seconds left on the clock. He's up on his seat, stomping and howling, his pounding footfalls vibrating the entire grandstand. The moms are all whispering among themselves. I don't have to guess what they're saying.

The game ends in a draw, but that means the Comets' play-off hopes are still alive. I can only imagine what he'll be like if they win the championship.

"What a game!" Dad raves when we're down on the field congratulating a triumphant Kristi. He turns to face me and adds, "You can't get this kind of excitement from planting onions!"

"Way to go, kid," I tell my sister. And I mean it. But I can't help reflecting that nothing I do is ever going to generate this much enthusiasm from our father. Not even if I grow a prize pumpkin that outweighs a Mini Cooper at the county fair.

Players and spectators are still swarming all over the field when one of the little brothers kicks a ball that whizzes past my head, barely missing me.

It triggers an instant memory. I'm in a room I don't recognize with another boy, who's stretched out on his bed, listening to headphones. I don't know him either. I guess he's not my biggest fan, though, because he throws a rock the size of a grapefruit at me. It sizzles past my ear, takes a divot out of the wall, and breaks in two. I gaze down at the pieces. It's some kind of geode. I can see purplish crystals in the middle. And this is the weirdest part: I know—I'm not sure how, but I do—that the kid stole it.

I guess I look stunned, because Kristi laughs at me. "It would have bounced off your head. So what?"

It takes me a second to realize she's talking about the soccer ball, not the geode.

For Dad, it's just another reminder of the athlete I'm not. His celebration is over.

As we climb into the car, my father and sister are reliving the entire game in a series of yammered play-by-plays. And me? My thoughts are in turmoil.

What room was that? What kid? What geode?

Most of all, why am I remembering things that never happened?

CHAPTER FIVE

REEF MOODY

The dent stares back at me from the wall of the bedroom I share with Declan.

How did it get there? I have absolutely no idea. It wasn't always there, was it?

Did I do it? It's right next to my bed. Like maybe I slammed my elbow into the wall one morning? But I'd remember that. And I'd definitely remember the trip to the emergency room for a busted funny bone and the six weeks with my arm in a cast.

I examine the damage carefully. It doesn't look like an elbow did it. The indentation is kind of round—a baseball? Or something a little bigger, like a softball? But it would have to have been a softball with little spikes, judging from the crumbling drywall and the dark scuffs in the paint.

Fact is, I just don't know. But it feels like I *should* know—and I can't quite explain that either. Because it's my side of the room, I'm afraid Willis and Jenna will blame it on me.

It's frustrating not to be able to remember . . . especially since I remember so many things I would love to forget. Like what happened to Mom, and the reason why I'm all alone in the world.

Too bad you don't get to pick what you remember. I wouldn't mind forgetting all the bad stuff, but instead I'm having trouble calling up a picture of my mother's smile or the way she looked at me when she was proud of something I did.

A thought occurs to me: Is forgetting what damaged the wall next to my bed the same as forgetting my mother's face? Are those things connected?

And what's really strange is that, at the same time as I'm doing all this forgetting, I'm also *remembering* extra things that never happened.

Lately, I've been googling phrases like *memory loss* and *false memory*, because I'm wondering if there might be a medical explanation for what I've been going through. And there are some diseases and conditions that mess with memory. Amnesia is the most famous, but I don't think I have it. Amnesia victims lose huge chunks of their lives; I'm only forgetting little bits and pieces. Plus, amnesia comes from something like an accident or an injury, and I haven't had anything like that. My head is too big to have made that dent in the wall. And even if it was the right size, where's the bump and the concussion?

Dementia is another condition they talk about on the internet, but that usually affects people sixty and older, so no way. There's even something called false memory syndrome, where people become totally convinced of things that never happened. I admit I'm a little worried about that one, but I don't think it applies to me either. According to the article I read, false memory syndrome isn't a real disease. The people who have it have been brainwashed, and I'm pretty sure that's not me. Besides, who would bother to brainwash a twelve-year-old kid so he remembers a rabbit and a bunch of plants?

Another memory that keeps coming to me is of a burly, dark-haired, middle-aged guy who never stops lecturing and nagging. I see him in several different poses, but what's common to all of them is that his mouth never stops. Strangely, even though he's always talking, I can't make out any words. It's just sounds, like the adults in Charlie Brown cartoons. Anyway, I don't want to know what he's saying. It's like he's judging me, and I'm getting a straight-F report card.

Something else that doesn't make sense: I call him Dad. That can't be right. I never knew my father.

At breakfast, Liam offers me a ride to school.

"You don't want Reek in your car!" Declan sneers. "He'll stink it up, just like he stinks up our house."

Carolyn groans into her cereal. "Leave the kid alone, Dec."

"I don't mind walking," I tell them. The last thing I need is to be squeezed into Liam's tiny car so Declan can elbow my ribs all the way to Delgado.

When I do make it to school, the day starts off on a rocky note. I'm on my way to homeroom when I find myself alone in the hall with Portia.

It should be no big deal. I see Portia all the time. I've even got a couple of classes with her. But this is different. We're meeting face-to-face, and there's nobody else around. No crowd to lose her in, no "distraction" so I can pretend I don't see her.

"Hi," I mumble.

She stops a few feet in front of me. "How are you, Reef?"

My heart sinks. It's not a casual greeting. It's a real question. She's nice. She honestly wants to know.

And I have an answer—just not one I can share with her. How can I ever tell her that I took her Covid and passed it along to my mother? That I have no life anymore, and even though it's not her fault, the roller coaster ride that brought me here started with her birthday party.

"I'm okay," I tell her, which isn't even a lie. I'm surviving. I'm as okay as I was yesterday and the day before that. And I'll probably be just as okay tomorrow. Not great, but okay.

She looks like she wants to say more. Like I mentioned, she's nice. We used to be friends. We *are* friends—in the sense that we never officially stopped. Things changed. *I* changed.

Some things that happen are so big you're never the same afterward.

I'm in Spanish class when the announcement comes on the PA system:

"Would Reef Moody report to the main office, please. Reef Moody to the office."

I can feel eyes burning into me from every other kid in the room. They're probably remembering the news I got the *last* time I was called to the office. Or maybe I'm just paranoid about being the center of attention. If there's one thing the kids in this school are good at, it's not caring about somebody else's lousy luck.

Is it just me, or is Señora Foster gazing at me in sympathy as I gather up my stuff and head out the door? I get the same looks from the secretaries as I report in at the office. They send me right in to see Principal Latimore.

I'm surprised to find Jenna seated across from the principal. Latimore seems ticked off, which is nothing new, since she's always ticked off. But then I see Jenna's face, and she's really upset.

"What's wrong?" I ask.

The principal indicates a stylish leather purse sitting on the desk. "Three days ago, my pocketbook was stolen from this office while everyone was out to lunch."

I'm a little confused, since the "stolen" pocketbook is sitting on the desk in front of us, not stolen at all.

Jenna takes up the tale. "I found it this morning. I was putting away laundry and it was in your sock drawer."

Guess I'm not that smart, because I blurt out the first thing that comes to my mind: "How would *her* pocketbook get into *my* sock drawer?"

Their expressions remain grim. That's when I clue in. "You think I took it?"

"The contents were undisturbed, including the credit cards," the principal goes on. "But the cash was gone—about two hundred dollars."

"I'm sorry you got robbed," I manage, "but it wasn't me!"

Jenna is practically in tears. "Oh, Reef! It was in your dresser! How else could it have gotten there?"

"Not by me!" I exclaim. I think it's pretty obvious who else could have done it—Declan. But how can I say that to Jenna?

And then I fall silent as a horrifying thought comes to me: The way my life has been going lately, I remember things that never happened and forget things that really did. How can I ever be one hundred percent sure that I didn't steal that pocketbook? I mean, I don't think I did. It's not like me to take something that isn't mine. I've never done it before; why would I start now?

But what if I'm wrong? What if stealing the principal's purse is one of the memories I've lost? What if I've done a lot of stealing in my life and conveniently forgotten it all? I could be twenty times worse than Declan and not even know.

They're both staring at me, so I have to say something. "What about the money, then?" I offer. "I should have two hundred dollars, and I don't. Or something I bought that cost two hundred dollars? Where's that?"

They don't answer. And the more I talk, the more I sound

like a guilty person throwing out excuses to explain away his crime.

"Why would I steal?" I'm almost pleading now. "Money won't buy what I need. You think I can get my mother back for two hundred bucks? If that was true, I absolutely would steal it—"

My voice cracks, so I shut up in a hurry, because if I go on any longer, I might start crying. And I'm not going to give them the satisfaction of seeing that.

The principal's expression is severe. "I know you've been through a lot, Reef. And I sympathize. We all do. But there are rules in life and laws in society. Stealing is never acceptable."

That's when Jenna assures me that I'm part of the Helmer family no matter what, so of course I'm not kicked out of the house. And that makes me feel even worse, because it means she thinks I'm guilty, and that stealing is the kind of thing that maybe you should get kicked out for.

I chomp down on the inside of my cheek until I taste blood. The pain doesn't exactly feel good, but it's the only thing that distracts me from how desperate I am.

Principal Latimore hands down my sentence. I'm not expelled or even suspended. I'm on probation. One more slipup and I'm gone. Also, I have to pay her back the two hundred bucks. So remember when I said I didn't need money? Scratch that. I need a lot.

"We can pay you to do odd jobs around the house," Jenna promises.

Why do I hate it so much when people are nice to me?

I walked into that office a normal kid. I walk out a thief. So much for innocent until proven guilty.

Or maybe I was proven guilty. The evidence was in my own sock drawer.

Wonder if I'm ever going to know the truth.

CHAPTER SIX

THEO METZINGER

I squeeze the spray bottle and lean forward to stick my nose into the puff of mist that comes out.

Yuck—that's awful. Not just a horrible smell, but strong and spicy too—the kind that goes right up your nasal passages and grabs you by the eye sockets, forcing tears to stream down your cheeks.

I try a different brand. God bless America, it's even worse! If I spray this stuff on my plants, the whole yard is going to stink to high heaven. The local neighborhood watch will vote us off the block, and who will blame them?

I'm in the garden center at Tools R Us, browsing through the different brands of rabbit repellent. If I can't keep Jaws away from our house, pretty soon there won't be any flowers or vegetables left. And judging by this rack, I'm not the only one with this problem. Who knew there were so many ways to rabbit-proof your garden? There's Rabbit Mace, Rabbit Bye-Bye, Deer and Rabbit Fence, Bunny Brigade, Hare-Today-Gone-Tomorrow—the list goes on and on.

A salesperson comes up behind me. "Can I help you, kid?"

"I'm looking for something to keep rabbits away, but these all smell so terrible," I complain.

"You're right. Rabbits respond to smell and taste, so these products work by making your garden not very appetizing anymore. But I'll let you in on a little secret: The best way to get rid of rabbits is urine."

I goggle. "You mean *pee*?"

He nods. "Works every time. Rabbits hate it. Makes them think there's a predator around, marking its territory."

Perfect. My parents already sent me to a psychiatrist. I don't want to know who I'll have to see if they catch me out in the yard, peeing on the vegetables. No one will ever believe that I'm rabbit-proofing.

"What's the second-best way to get rid of rabbits?" I ask.

The guy looks around furtively. "You didn't hear this from me," he half whispers, "but you don't need any of these fancy products. Just mix up a batch of the stinkiest stuff at your house—vinegar, Tabasco, garlic powder, cayenne pepper. Add water, boil it up on the stove, and when it cools, spray the liquid on your plants. Problem solved."

So I race home and do exactly that. I even add a few extra ingredients. Mom likes to experiment with recipes from around the world, so we have things like chili oil, crushed habanero peppers, and gochujang paste. When it boils in our biggest pasta pot, my eyes start burning so badly that I have to leave the kitchen. And I protect my face with a towel when I go back in to turn off the burner and let my creation cool.

I lower the towel just in time to see my father reaching a cooking spoon into the pot and drawing a taste to his lips.

Before I can yell *"Don't!"* it's down the hatch, and my

father is doing something I can only describe as levitating. He leaps around the kitchen like a prima ballerina, spitting and screaming.

"What the—" He says a lot more, but his voice gives out on him, and all I can hear is guttural throat-clearing that reminds me of a chain saw cutting into a piece of metal.

I pour him a big glass of milk and he manages to gulp it all down. When he's done, he gasps out, "What *was* that?"

"Rabbit repellent," I explain.

"Rabbit repellent? Why would Mom be cooking—" It finally dawns on him that what he tasted wasn't dinner. But knowing what it is makes him even madder. "Rabbit repellent," he repeats in a calmer tone. "For your rabbit."

"Jaws," I admit sheepishly.

In answer, he takes my concoction off the stove and pours it down the sink.

"Dad! I was going to use that!"

"You won't need it," he assures me. "You can't repel a rabbit like that. You've got to take him on, man to man."

I have to snicker. "You mean man to hare?"

"Don't get smart with me. I'm going to settle this once and for all. That rabbit is going down."

When I was little, and my father first told me how he ruled the school, I always pictured him dressed like a king, with a crown and velvet robes, haranguing his loyal subjects on bleachers in a gym, with basketball hoops at each end.

But watching him go after Jaws makes me revise that picture. Now it's almost military, making snares out of sticks and fishing line, and setting out Brussels sprouts and lettuce as rabbit bait.

Wouldn't you know it—Kristi thinks this is fun and appoints herself his assistant. As he's deploying the snares all around the yard, she shows up with a pair of binoculars so they can hide in our tree house and wait for the enemy to show himself.

Mom appears beside me at the open kitchen window. "Looks like they're having fun. You should go out and join them."

I shake my head. "I refuse to have any part in this."

But when I see the flash of brown fur that tells me Jaws is paying a visit to the garden, I can't look away. Is this going to be the end of my epic struggle against The Rabbit From the Black Lagoon?

What happens next is hard to describe, except to say it's a shame I didn't film it on my phone. It would have gotten fifty million views on YouTube, easy.

Jaws dashes around the yard, helping himself to every single piece of bait but somehow avoiding the snares, kicking them down with his big, flat feet.

"Daddy, the traps aren't working!" I hear my sister exclaim.

In an echo of the athlete he used to be, my father crawls

out of the tree house and whooshes face-first down the slide, landing on his feet in a spectacular somersault at the bottom. As Jaws streaks past, Dad lunges at him in a diving tackle, just grazing the long ears. I watch bug-eyed as the rabbit scoots out from between meaty hands and disappears under the fence into the neighbor's yard.

I swallow a "Yippee!" that's already halfway out my mouth.

Dad storms over to the house, his face a thundercloud. "What are you cheering about, mister? This is supposed to be for you."

He's got a point. All he's trying to do is to protect my plants from that marauding bunny, and here I am, rooting for the enemy. I can't really explain it. I want Jaws out of the garden more than anybody. I wouldn't even mind if he helped himself to the occasional carrot or petunia, but that's not his style. He takes a little nibble of everything out there, so it's all ruined. No question about it: The rabbit has to go.

Still, seeing him out there, defeating so many snares while still managing to snag the bait—you've got to admire the little guy's sheer courage. He took on a two-hundred-pound man who used to rule a school and *won*.

"Sorry, Dad," I mumble.

He's not in a forgiving mood. "I'll never understand what makes you tick! I'm trying to help you out—you and your flowers and your plants. But nothing I do will ever be good enough for you."

That startles me, because I've had the same thought myself at least fifty times . . . about him. Nothing *I* do will ever be good enough for Dad.

And right there, peering through the window screen at my father, I have another one of those strange memories of something that never happened. I'm standing opposite a kid who's scowling just like Dad. We're close—uncomfortably close—right in each other's faces. I can sense the anger in the memory. This is a confrontation.

I don't know him, but to my surprise, I realize that, in a way, I do. He was in that other false recollection, the kid who threw the geode at me.

"You'll pay for that," he promises darkly.

The picture is so immediate, so fresh, that it almost feels like my father just threatened me. But no—he's already walking away, stooping to pick up the flattened snares.

Kristi sidles up to me at the window. "Don't tell Dad," she whispers, "but I was cheering for the rabbit too."

CHAPTER SEVEN

REEF MOODY

Question: How do you earn two hundred dollars to pay back your principal?

Answer: Garbage.

That's what Willis and Jenna come up with. I am now officially in charge of garbage at the Helmer household. It's an awesome responsibility, but somebody has to do it. And it's a fitting punishment for the pocketbook I didn't steal—or maybe I did. When you can't trust your own memory, you're not exactly in a position to complain about how unfair it is.

I'm not even joking about the responsibility. You wouldn't believe how big an operation garbage is in this house. There are dinner dishes to be scraped, wastebaskets to be emptied, recycling to be collected and sorted. Everything has to be bagged and put in the cans, and the cans dragged to the curb on garbage day, then dragged back and hosed out, so they don't start to stink. It's gross, but at least it's boring too. For this, Willis and Jenna pay me twenty bucks a week. That means I'll be free of my debt to Principal Latimore by Christmas.

I'm struggling along the walkway with the last bag of the

day when I notice that my heavy burden is getting light. This can only mean one thing: Declan has cut another hole in the plastic, and I'm slowly losing my load. An over-the-shoulder glance confirms it. The trail of garbage stretches all the way back to the front porch.

Eggshells. Why do there always have to be eggshells? They're slimy and they break into a million pieces when you try to pick them up.

A loud cackling from above shatters the quiet of the evening. I look up. Declan's big, unruly head sticks out of our window. He's checking out his handiwork and having a good laugh at my expense. It's partly his revenge for the kick that put him on his butt in the upstairs hall, but it's mostly because he's just plain rotten. Willis and Jenna assume that I'm too clumsy to get a bag as far as the cans without breaking it. It never dawns on them that I'm a victim of sabotage. And how can I rat their darling son out? He belongs here and I don't.

"Nice," I call up to him.

"Now you really are Reek." He leers down at me. "And thanks to you, the whole front of the house reeks too."

So I pick up the mess. Sometimes I also have to hose down the walk, but today's not that bad—no gravy or sauces or anything like that. Then, just as I'm stuffing everything into a fresh bag, I'm suddenly surrounded by a blizzard of white flakes. Snow? It's seventy degrees outside!

That's when I notice that Declan is dumping a bucket of torn paper confetti down on me.

I shake my fist at him. "This isn't *my* garbage! It's *your* garbage!"

"It's *all* your garbage, Reek," he shoots back at me with a smarmy grin.

And he's right. It isn't fair; it's just true. Fact is, there's only one garbage specialist at the Helmer house, and it's me.

Takes some doing, but eventually I get all those scraps into a third bag that I cram into the can. I'm finally making for the front door when I veer off the walk and head out into the street. I need a shower, but not as much as I need to be away from that place. Away from Declan, sure, but also away from a family that gives me no choice but to take this from him. Willis and Jenna don't see it, but that's mostly because they don't want to see it. And Liam and Carolyn just plain don't care.

I walk until the cobwebs clear out of my brain and the garbage smell disappears from my nostrils. I'm just drifting, putting one foot in front of the other, but part of me already knows what the destination is going to be. I'm not far from Delgado now, on the main drag of stores and restaurants where the teachers all run errands during free periods.

Pretty soon, I'm standing directly in front of it, like I've been led here by GPS: the Willow Street branch of the Trident Federal Credit Union and Bank. I come here a lot, and not just because it's close to my school. This is where Mom used to work. She was a loan officer, and a teller before that.

When I was with friends, I used to take the long way home

from school just to avoid passing here and seeing her at her desk in the window. Thought it was embarrassing, I guess. Now I wish I could go back in time so I could walk by the branch every single day. I'd even wave to her.

Then again, if I could go back in time, I'd make sure I didn't go anywhere near Portia's birthday party and everything would be different.

Trident has those old-fashioned teller cages. Before she got her own office, Mom used to joke that she felt like a parrot, and was tempted to squawk *"Polly want a cracker!"* at customers at the end of a long day. I try to picture her there in the half-light of the closed branch.

And I can't.

I stand stock-still on the sidewalk. The thing where I can't conjure up my mother's face has been getting worse. It doesn't throw me into blind panic anymore, but this is almost more terrible. It's like I'm not fighting it. I've accepted that this is the way it's going to be from now on. She'll get dimmer and dimmer until she just sort of winks out. And what happens after that? Once her image has disappeared, what will I forget next? Her voice? The things she said to me over the years? And with everything about her gone, will I forget she even existed? Sure, I'll have Jenna to tell me things about her, but that's not the same as *remembering*. That's like school, where you learn about the Stamp Act or World War Two. I'll forget her as surely as I forgot how the wall over my bed got damaged.

If there's anywhere my mother's face should come back to

me, it's here at this bank, where she worked for years. I have no connection to this place that isn't Mom-related. And still she's nowhere to be found. I concentrate so hard that my strength gives out and I collapse into a cross-legged heap on the sidewalk. I bring her back, just for a second. But it's not the real her. It's the picture from my nightstand, the one with the broken frame. There's Mom, with a sharp crack cutting straight through her smile.

No! I scramble to my feet. I refuse to let this happen. I scrunch up my face and focus so intently that the name reverberates inside my head: *Mom . . . Mom . . . Mom . . .*

A memory does come—from way back. I'm a little kid. I know this because I have to reach way up to hold her hand. I see caves and water and ice floes. Penguins waddle around, alone and in groups, splashing and swimming.

The penguin exhibit at the zoo!

I loved the zoo. Even though we didn't have a lot of money, we always bought a family membership so we could go as often as we wanted. And the penguin exhibit was always my favorite.

I feel happy and excited, but I'm not sure if that's part of the memory or if I'm just triumphant because I remember.

I look up at her . . . and get the shock of a lifetime. *The woman holding my hand is not my mother.*

I reach out and steady myself against a mailbox. It's not her. It isn't even like her. Mom's hair was fair and straight. This lady's cheeks are fuller, and she has dark curly hair. I've never seen her before in my life.

But in the memory, I'm not freaking out or pulling away. I'm acting like everything's totally fine and I belong with this stranger.

She says, "Aren't they adorable, Theo?"

Theo? Who's Theo?

CHAPTER EIGHT

THEO METZINGER

You'd think a grown man could forgive a rabbit for making him look bad.

Think again.

My father is out to get Jaws, no matter what the cost. I'm supposed to be grateful for this, because he started doing it for me, to protect my plants.

He isn't doing it for me anymore.

Now it's personal.

The backyard is a minefield. You can't take three steps without tripping over one of Dad's homemade traps, which are basically plastic buckets balanced on Popsicle sticks. I've already had to release two squirrels, a chipmunk, and a sparrow. The sparrow had hard feelings about being caught. It flapped in my face before flying off in a snit.

"Can't we take the traps away?" my mother pleads. "They're an eyesore. And they're obviously not working."

"They're working perfectly," my father insists. "We're catching things."

"Just not the rabbit," Kristi points out.

"His day will come," Dad growls. "And sooner than you think."

To be honest, I'm starting to wonder about that. I know rabbits aren't supposed to be very smart, but Jaws might be the Einstein of the species, or at least the Houdini. He's definitely gifted when it comes to avoiding snares and traps. And in the meantime, he's helped himself to a lot of Brussels sprouts, lettuce, carrots, and kale Dad set out as bait. Sometimes Jaws leaves the kale. Now I'm positive he's smart. Nobody likes kale.

Mom complains about the wasted vegetables. But if the goal is keeping Jaws out of my garden, mission accomplished. There's so much food sitting out under the buckets that Jaws hasn't touched my plants in days. He's probably as stuffed as a little kid the morning after Halloween. And since I don't have to worry about the garden anymore, I'm starting to look at the rabbit with admiration and maybe even a little affection. After all, you have to appreciate any critter who can take on a guy who once ruled his school!

When Dad comes back from Tools R Us with a store-bought trap called the Rabbit Defender, I'm not worried at all. Jaws made it this far. My money's on him.

I'm in my room after karate on Tuesday when my father's voice reaches me from the yard.

"Gotcha!"

I rush to the window in time to see him holding up the Rabbit Defender in triumph. This thing is no do-it-yourself job with buckets and Popsicle sticks. It looks professional—strong metal bars and a spring-loaded mechanism that locks the intruder into the cage the instant the bait is touched. Trapped inside is a bundle of gray-brown fur: Jaws.

When the rabbit was ransacking my plants and, later, outsmarting Dad at every turn, he was somehow larger in my imagination, growing into the folk hero I was making him in my mind. But now, he's never seemed smaller, like a terrified sock puppet darting around the confined space.

When I pound downstairs and burst through the back door, a horrifying sight greets my eyes. Dad has Jaws out of the cage and is holding him by the head and midsection, about to wring his little neck. The rabbit's back legs kick wildly in desperation.

"Dad! You can't—"

He shoots me the half-disappointed, half-disgusted expression I always get when I've failed some toughness trial I didn't know about. "Come on, Theo, what did you think was going to happen? You don't have to watch this, but it would probably be a good lesson. The whole world isn't pretty flowers—"

And I know he's going to do it. He's going to kill that poor rabbit. My rabbit, my fault—if it wasn't for my gardening, Dad never would have known Jaws existed.

All at once, another memory comes at me. I see manicured lawns, expert landscaping. A park? A golf course?

The next image slams into me with the force of a battering ram.

A coffin!

This is a funeral!

Before I have a chance to wonder why I'm there or who died, a sadness comes over me that's heavier, more devastating than anything I've ever experienced before. I can't think; in the memory, I can't breathe. I'm not even crying; I'm choking. It's like I'm underwater. All I want is air.

And just as suddenly, the dream is gone and I'm springing into action, hurling myself at my father. I'm fully airborne as I bring my arm down onto Dad's wrist. It's an elbow smash from karate—a *hiza-ate*—but while it's happening, I'm not thinking about that. I'm not thinking at all. It's pure instinct.

With a cry of shock, Dad loses his grip on Jaws, and the little guy goes flying. I'll bet Jaws is shocked too—but not so much that he can't take advantage of this lucky break. He hits the ground running, executes a couple of wobbly circles to get his bearings, and takes off like a missile. In seconds, he's under the fence to the neighbor's yard, and gone.

I resist cheering, because I know I'm in big trouble now. By the time I'm through being grounded over this, I'll be tripping over my own beard.

"You hit me!" Dad exclaims in wonder.

I try to apologize. But it doesn't really come off, because I'm so obviously not sorry. I wanted to save Jaws and I succeeded. That's pretty plain.

"Who taught you how to do that?" he demands.

"It's . . . a karate move." Now I'm really toast. The first rule Sensei taught us is that you never use martial arts against anyone in the real world. It's a discipline, a sport. "I promise I'll never do it again!"

"Yeah, okay, good," he approves. As he walks into the

house, he tosses the Rabbit Defender into the trash. His back is to me, but I think his cheeks are sticking out.

He's *smiling*!

Wouldn't you know it? His well-behaved son, who follows every rule, is never good enough for him. And now that I finally do something awful—to *him*—he's proud of me.

I can't wait to hear what Dr. Abagnale is going to say about this.

I'm alone in the yard and cold reality swamps me. I probably won't be able to talk about this with Dr. Abagnale at all. Then I'd have to tell her what put me into attack mode in the first place—the funeral memory that came on so suddenly.

I've never been to a funeral. I've never even seen a coffin except on TV. But the psychiatrist doesn't want to hear about that. She thinks "our" mind is suffering from information overload.

Maybe she's right. She's the doctor, after all. But how could I forget a *funeral*? The feeling of overpowering grief comes back to me, and my knees almost buckle. It's like I was a *mourner* at this funeral. Which would mean I lost someone important in my life. But who?

I do a quick inventory: Mom, Dad, Kristi. Grandparents on both sides. Nobody's missing.

Unless—this sounds pretty bananas, but what other explanation could there be?—the person I lost is from a part of my life I've forgotten.

I know it makes no sense. Still, somehow, I've got to work this out.

"I heard you punched Dad in the face today," Kristi snickers at the dinner table that night.

I feel my cheeks burning. "It was just his arm. And it wasn't a punch. It was *hiza-ate*."

Dad rolls up his sleeve to reveal a black-and-purple bruise on his wrist. "It was quite a shot," he chortles.

Mom looks disapproving. "I hope you apologized."

"I did! I wasn't trying to hurt anybody. I just couldn't let him kill the rabbit."

Dad has a different interpretation. "You saw what you wanted and you made it happen. That's what men do."

"And girls," Kristi adds.

She and Dad exchange a fist bump.

I leap suddenly to my feet, overturning my chair. From the table, I can see the kitchen TV, which is muted. The local news is on, showing three fire department pumpers spraying water on a low, sprawling factory with flames shooting out of the roof.

"Theo, what's wrong?" my mother asks in concern.

Speechless, I point at the screen.

She nods gravely. "That happened this afternoon. It's over now, but the whole building burned to the ground."

She thinks I'm looking at the fire. I'm not. As the news shows an aerial view of the action, I can see a panorama of roofs through the billowing gray smoke. One of them, in the distance, shows a white cupola atop a dark brick building.

I *know* that place.

No, that's wrong. I don't know it; I *remember* it. Actually, I don't really remember it either. But my memory says I do. I distinctly remember walking out of that school, where the floor tiles were wrong, and seeing that cupola up on the roof.

The story ends and the news broadcast switches to a commercial.

"Where was that fire?" I ask urgently.

"Don't worry," Mom soothes me. "It wasn't anywhere near here."

"But *where*?" I demand.

"On the south side somewhere," Dad supplies. "What do you care, Theo? It's over. The building's gone. Bad things happen sometimes."

They sure do. And weird things happen too.

I *remember* being inside that school with the cupola on the roof. And now, here, on my own TV, in my own kitchen, is proof positive that school is a real place. I never went there. We've always lived on the west side. But the memory—that has to be real, almost like I had a secret life that I've somehow forgotten, and it's coming back to me in bits and pieces.

One thing's for sure: I need to find that school. It could be the key to understanding what's been happening to me. If I could get myself there, walk those halls with the wrong tiles, maybe talk to some of the students, it could go a long way to solving this mystery.

After dinner, I head upstairs to my computer and do a search for *factory fire* coupled with today's date. It comes right up: the Amalgamated Printpack Company, which manufactured folding cartons for games and toys. I take the address and plug it into a city map. The exact location comes up: a neighborhood called Breezeway just south of downtown.

According to the navigation app, it's 4.6 miles away.

Not exactly around the corner, but very doable by bike.

CHAPTER NINE

REEF MOODY

I spot the police car the instant I step around the corner to the Helmers' block.

There are a lot of houses on our side of the street, but I *know* the cops have come for me.

It's so unfair. Latimore got her purse back. And she's getting her cash back as fast as I can earn it—it's not my fault Willis and Jenna think garbage duty is only worth twenty bucks a week.

Why the cops? Why *now*?

My first impulse is to run. I don't have to go home. That's not my home anyway, and the Helmers are definitely not my family.

I actually take a few steps in the opposite direction before I pull up short. Where am I going to go? To live on the lam as a twelve-year-old fugitive because of two hundred bucks that maybe I didn't even steal?

I bounce on the sidewalk, shifting my weight from one foot to the other. Every time I think my situation can't possibly get any worse, I always turn out to be wrong.

As I watch, the front door opens and two cops emerge. I'm

rooted to the spot. Should I run? Hide? It's time for action, but for some reason, I can't move.

The two officers get into their car and drive away. They don't even glance at me as they pass by.

I begin to breathe again, but now I'm confused. If they weren't here to arrest me, why were the police at the Helmer place? It probably wasn't for a taste of Jenna's famous apple strudel.

Still scared but mostly curious now, I jog to the house and let myself in. All five Helmers are in the living room. Willis and Jenna are standing over Declan, who is seated in a straight-back chair, his arms folded tightly across his chest. His expression is a mixture of anger and pure sulk, his cheeks the color of pickled beets. It tells me one thing instantly: The cops weren't here because of me. They were here because of Declan.

"What's up?" I ask.

From Declan's perspective, that's the wrong thing to say. "Shut up, Reek! You're not even part of this family!"

Carolyn mutters, "I wish *I* wasn't part of this family."

"Calm down, everybody," Willis orders.

I press. "There were two cops in here. What was that all about?"

Declan begins to rise out of his seat like a guided missile, but his father shoves him back down.

Jenna casts me an exasperated look. "You of all people should show a little understanding. None of us are perfect."

Compared to Declan, Jack the Ripper is perfect. I think it, but I'd never dare say it out loud. It's pretty obvious what happened. Their darling son got himself arrested. It obviously wasn't the crime of the century, since those two cops brought him home and left him with his parents. But I'll bet this isn't over. I can tell by the way they're looking at me that they're waiting for me to buzz off so they can finish talking this out.

"I've got homework," I mumble, and head for the stairs.

Nobody stops me. I climb the steps slowly, hoping to overhear something. No such luck. No one says a word until they hear my door close.

So what? It makes absolutely no difference to me to know how Declan got himself arrested. Being nosy is what a little brother would do.

I'm not Declan's brother, and that's the way I like it.

But the minute I sit down on my bed, I notice something. Wanda is gone—not a person; the electronic personal assistant Declan has had on his desk the last couple of days. He'd ask "her" the answers to homework questions and get her to play music for him. Mostly, though, he'd curse her out, and she'd reply, "I'm sorry, Declan, I don't know what that word means." Declan got a big kick out of that.

There was always something fishy about Wanda's presence in our room. It wasn't a holiday; it wasn't Declan's birthday; and for sure he didn't do anything extra good to deserve a bonus gift. Declan stole Wanda and it took the police a couple of days to identify his face in the security camera footage.

That's my roommate. Quality guy.

Of course, I can't help but think that the Wanda isn't the only thing Declan stole lately. There's the little matter of the principal's pocketbook. And if my memory wasn't so messed up lately, I'd feel a lot more definite about that. If I can forget my own mother's face, I can forget anything.

But definite or not, without proof, I don't dare make an accusation like that.

Why would anyone in this house believe me?

After dinner, I swing into my role as the Helmer house's one-man garbage squad, but when I go to empty the upstairs wastebaskets, they've been cleaned out. In the kitchen, the dirty plates are gone from the sink, and the dishwasher is already running. The bin where we collect recyclables is nowhere to be seen.

I head to the garage just in time to see Declan staggering under the weight of two enormous Hefty bags. But when he tries to grab the metal recycling bin under his elbow, bag number two slips. And as he squats to pick it up, the bin tilts over, dumping cans and plastic bottles all over the concrete floor.

I scramble to gather some of the fallen cans and toss them back in with the others.

"Beat it, Reek!" he snaps, dropping everything to confront me. "You think you can swipe my credit for doing this?"

"What credit?" I retort. "Garbage is *my* job. I need the money so I can pay back Latimore!"

"Not my problem." He hefts the two bags and freezes me with a furious look. "Don't touch that bin. I'll be back for it in a second."

He opens the garage door and starts down the driveway to the curb.

I finish loading up the recycling and follow him down the driveway.

"What did I tell you?" He swings one of the bags at me, missing my nose by half an inch in a very fragrant flyby. "It's *my* house, so it's *my* garbage!" He actually snickers a little at that—the first time I've ever known Declan to display a sense of humor. He sours quickly, though, and adds, "And it's *my* parents who are making me do this."

I keep my firm grip on the recyclables. "Stinks to be you, I guess." I march past him and set the bin down by the curb.

He thinks it over and finally nods. "Stinks to be both of us."

He drops the garbage next to the recycling, and we return to the house in silence.

CHAPTER TEN

THEO METZINGER

The next morning, Dad catches me pulling my bike out of the garage when I should be at the end of the block, waiting for the school bus.

"I figured I'd ride today," I tell him. "I need more exercise."

He nods approvingly. "Good call. Nice to see you taking an interest in something besides digging in the yard."

I take that personally, but I'm not going to make a big deal out of it to my father. Today isn't about exercise anyway. It's about getting to Breezeway and finding that cupola.

All day at school, I'm jumpy and nervous. Okay, 4.6 miles isn't exactly globe-trotting. But in a city like ours, it will take me through a lot of different areas I don't know. Plus, I think I'm probably going to have to cut last period, which isn't something I've ever done before. It's Friday, so I don't have karate or Dr. Abagnale. But who knows how long it's going to take to navigate through all those strange neighborhoods? Plus, I have specific directions to the factory that burned down, but not to that school. Once I'm in Breezeway, I should be able to spot the cupola, but what if I can't? I'll have no choice but to ride up and down random streets, hoping to find it by pure chance.

Yeah, I know. I overthink. Dr. Abagnale tells me that all the time—although when she says it, it's always "*we* overthink."

I'm definitely overthinking as I make my way through the crowded halls in the passing period after eighth hour. Is it just me or is it obvious that everybody else is moving on to another class and I'm sneaking out of the building? I wedge myself into the alcove of a drinking fountain and wait until the rush subsides a little. Then I'm out the door like a shot, fumbling the combination of my bike lock, hopping up on the seat, and pedaling for freedom.

As the building passes out of view behind me, I experience a rush of exhilaration I'm not used to. Maybe this is how it feels to "rule the school" or at least break the rules. I have to admit it's a new sensation and not necessarily a bad one. It mixes with determination as I turn onto the main road and head south.

My bike has a front basket—not very cool, I know; it's one of the reasons I never ride to school. I put it on to carry gardening supplies, but now it comes in handy because I'm navigating on my phone. It bounces a lot, so it's hard to focus on the screen. But there are also voice directions, so I always have some idea of where I'm supposed to go.

A couple of construction detours take me out of my way, and I get held up at a train crossing and a series of busy intersections with heavy traffic. About half an hour in, I can add an extra navigation system to the phone app: my nose. There's an acrid smoky smell to the air, and it seems to be getting stronger.

I've been riding for about forty minutes when I pull up to the Amalgamated Printpack factory—what's left of it, anyway.

Most of the building has collapsed, and what's still standing is blackened beyond all recognition. The smell is so strong it makes me gag.

Eagerly, I scan the horizon. My heart sinks. No cupola. It was easy to spot on the TV news, since the camera angle was from a helicopter. But here on the ground, you can't see very far.

My rear end is already aching from too much time on the bike seat, but I get back on and start to explore the neighborhood, keeping my gaze at rooftop level. I don't find the cupola, but I do make a discovery that's even more amazing. I *know* this place. The stores—they're familiar to me. That dry cleaner—I definitely recognize the writing on their sign! But how is that possible? I've never been to Breezeway before!

And that bank! Almost on autopilot, I hit the brakes and my bike shudders to a stop in front of a branch of Trident Credit Union. Through the window, I can see a man sitting at a desk, but I *remember* a lady in that office—slim, with light brown hair. I can picture her face as clearly as if she was standing right in front of me. Weirder still, for some reason I *want* her to be there. The yearning is so powerful it's almost a physical ache. Why? She seems vaguely familiar, but I don't understand how I ever could have met her.

As I stand there, wondering what my next move should be, a couple of kids my age round the corner and head up the main drag. They're carrying backpacks. A quick check of my phone confirms that it's just after three thirty, prime school dismissal time. It hits me—the place I'm looking for is a school! Another group comes into view. Two of them wear T-shirts emblazoned with DELGADO MIDDLE SCHOOL. That must be it!

I climb on the bike and ride in the direction the kids are coming from. As I coast down the block, the crowd thickens into a parade. I'm convinced I'm on the right track. Some of the faces even look sort of familiar—which, again, should be impossible. But if I can recognize a dry cleaner or a bank, why not people?

I wheel around one more corner and there it is: the cupola, just the way I remember it . . . except I shouldn't remember it at all. At first, it peeks out over a row of storefronts, but as I get closer, the whole place comes into view.

School must have just let out for the day, and kids are filing onto buses lined up along the circular drive. There are the brickwork steps that seemed so wrong in my memory because I knew they didn't belong at the entrance of my own school. Now I understand why. They *aren't* at my own school; they're here.

Eventually, the buses pull away, leaving a handful of students milling around in front of the building. I get off my bike and lean it against the playground fence. I don't know what my plan is, but I came to find this place and here I am. What's the next step? Am I waiting for one of the locals to point at me and yell, "Hey, that's the guy who used to go here, but he got amnesia, and his parents didn't tell him about it, because . . . because . . ." I can't imagine how the rest of that sentence might go.

That would make things a lot easier, but nobody comes

running to welcome back a long-lost classmate. I've accomplished my goal—I've found the school with the cupola. That's as far as it goes, though.

And then *she* comes out the front entrance and down the steps, passing so close to me that I could reach out and touch her. In Breezeway, a lot of the faces ring a bell, but with her, the bell is as loud as a cherry bomb. At the sight of her, dozens of memories pop into my head. We're obviously friends, but there must be more to it than that. There's an importance to our connection, a weight. I can even access her name.

"Portia!" I blurt.

She looks startled. "Are you talking to me?"

She doesn't know me! Why not? I know her! In a split second, I understand that Portia and I are *not* friends. She's never laid eyes on me in her life.

"Oh—uh—" I keep my panic under control. What can I do? Pretend to be talking to somebody else? How many Portias can there be?

She goes on. "You don't go to school here. How do you know my name?"

There's an answer to that question, but not one I could ever present to her. Memories of Portia whirl around my head, offering fleeting glimpses. Most of them take place at a school—probably this one. But I can't claim to be her classmate at Delgado. She's already concluded that I'm a stranger here.

I get another image—Portia behind a counter, handing out boxes of groceries. Mentally, I zoom in on the logo on the carton: NEIGHBORHOOD HARVEST FOOD BANK.

"From the food bank!" I exclaim.

Her eyes narrow. "I don't remember seeing you there."

My mind races. "I volunteer on the delivery trucks. We've made a couple of shipments here. I'm Theo." I hold out my hand.

She shakes it. "Oh, hi. Sorry—I meet a lot of people at the food bank. It's hard to keep all the faces straight."

It makes instant sense that people remember Portia more than vice versa. When she smiles at me, it's like the sun comes out from behind a cloud, bathing all of Delgado in bright light. Hers is not the kind of face anybody forgets.

For once, I wish I was more like my father. Dad could have a two-hour conversation with a Tasmanian devil, and by the end of it, they'd be best buddies. That's part of Rule the School—you always have total confidence that everyone wants to hear what you have to say, because you're you. I'm kind of the opposite of that. Mom claims I'm destined to be the strong, silent type, but mostly I'm just silent. Okay, I'm shy—especially when it comes to talking to girls. Maybe that's why I'm into gardening. Onions don't need much in the way of conversation.

"Do you live around here?" Portia asks.

"Not far." I gesture over my shoulder in the direction of home. Portia doesn't have to know that it's on another side of town. The circumference of the Earth is about 25,000 miles, so 4.6 counts as "not far." To keep the conversation going, I say, "Whenever I'm in the neighborhood, I always stop by. I think the cupola on the school roof is really cool."

No sooner are the words out of my mouth than I know I've said something boring and stupid. People who rule a school don't care about architecture.

She glances up. "*Cupola*—is that what you call that thing?" And just to double prove that the topic interests her zero percent, she adds, "Well, bye. Happy, uh, looking at the roof."

I'm not sure why, but I'm convinced this is a big moment. Portia is my only solid connection to the memories that aren't really memories. If I let her leave now, who knows if I'll ever be able to find her again.

I have to say something else to keep this going. What, though? I'm not my father. I'm not a schmoozer. I hang out with cucumbers, not with girls like Portia. I want to talk but my mind is a black hole.

She starts away. It's now or never. What would Dad do? If I knew the answer to that, I probably wouldn't disappoint him fifteen times a day.

I remember his words from the time I went after him to save Jaws: *You saw what you wanted and you made it happen . . .*

I match Portia step by step, walking my bike along the sidewalk. I feel like a doofus, not to mention a total stalker. I'll bet my cheeks are bright red.

She glances at my bike and grins. "Nice basket."

I stick out my jaw. "During planting season, I can get twelve small pots in there."

She laughs in my face. "Theo, you're hilarious."

Her destination turns out to be a shop called Fro-Yo Joe's. I'm not invited, but, following the Dad reasoning—*Who waits to be invited? You just go*—I'm also not *not* invited. So I lean my bike against the outside wall and wander in with her. She doesn't complain.

So far, so good.

Fro-Yo Joe's is mostly filled with Delgado kids slurping desserts and shoveling toppings. Everybody seems to know Portia. They practically break their necks to welcome her and be noticed. I'm starting to suspect that Portia is another one of those people who rule the school. Maybe that's why Dad logic seems to work with her.

"This is Theo," she introduces me.

It's pathetic how honored I am that she remembers my name.

For a shy kid like me to be thrust into a bustling crowd of strangers who all know each other is the definition of uncomfortable. I buy myself a small cone and hide behind it as best I can, but everybody seems to want to know who is this outsider who's suddenly friends with Portia. My usual companions—green peppers and daisies—are satisfied with water and a little fertilizer every now and then. Middle schoolers, not so much. It only makes it weirder that so many of these kids are familiar. At one point, I actually smear fro-yo on my chin so I can disappear behind a napkin for a while.

While I'm cleaning myself up, another face appears at the window. It gives me a jolt. If some of the people in Fro-Yo Joe's ring a bell, this newcomer is definitely a guy I know. He has a serious expression, and his eyes are distant and sad.

Why do I recognize this person? How do I know him?

He's already gone by the time I have the answer. And anyway, my answer doesn't make much sense. It's another memory: I'm washing up in a school bathroom. And when I clear the soap and water from my eyes, *his* is the face that's looking back at me from the mirror.

Like he's *me*.

Except how could he be?

CHAPTER ELEVEN

REEF MOODY

I'm off the garbage squad. Got fired.

It shouldn't bug me so much, since I hated doing the garbage. But it does. Fact is, I don't like losing to Declan, even if it's the worst job in the world. Mom used to tell me that, in the business world, you'll never beat the person who has connections, and Willis and Jenna are Declan's parents. You can't get more connected than that.

Things would be a little more bearable if I was off the hook for the two hundred bucks, but I'm not. They just switched me to a different job: vacuuming. It pays the same amount, but it's a lot harder, because it never ends. At least when you take the garbage out, it's out. With vacuuming, it's only as clean as the last slob to walk across the carpet. The kitchen is even worse.

Plus, now that Declan knows I'm vacuuming, he deliberately steps in mud so he can track it all over the house. Then he complains about what a lousy job I'm doing and how I shouldn't get paid.

That's not the worst thing he's doing. I'm positive he's cutting up straight pins and spreading the pieces all around the carpets. When the machine sucks them up, they tear holes in the dust bag. So when I open up to change bags, all I get is a giant cloud of powdery grime and fuzz, which goes all over the floor again. Now Jenna thinks I'm too stupid to change a vacuum bag without making a mess. And I can't tell her it's Declan's fault, because it's yet another thing I can't prove.

Another side effect of my new job: It's triggering a whole fresh round of fake memories. These usually involve me pushing a lawn mower around a yard, but sometimes it's a spreader, like for fertilizer or grass seed. That might go along with all those gardening memories I've had, but it's just not me. Mom and I were apartment people, so there was no lawn to take care of. And here at the Helmers', Willis does all the lawn care work. He says it relaxes him. Willis needs to relax. He's Declan's father. And to be fair, it can't be easy to inherit a whole extra kid because your wife's best friend happens to die.

I get paid on the weekend. So every Monday morning, I go to the office before the bell rings and give Principal Latimore a twenty-dollar bill. Right now, I've paid sixty bucks toward my debt. The principal said it was okay for me to save up and give her the whole two hundred at the end. But I live with Declan, which means no hiding place short of Fort Knox will ever be safe enough.

Latimore is always super businesslike. She takes my twenty

and writes me a receipt on her FROM THE DESK OF PRINCIPAL LATIMORE notepad. "So you'll always have proof that you paid," she explains.

"I trust you."

The look on her face clearly says that the feeling is definitely not mutual. It doesn't fill me with a warm, joyful feeling, that's for sure. But I have to admit she's been pretty cool about this whole thing.

The big news at school is that Portia supposedly has a new boyfriend, this kid they call Basket Case. Some people are saying he isn't a real boyfriend, just "some guy who might maybe one day turn into a boyfriend." Considering that the seventh graders at Delgado date and break up every time the wind blows, you'd think this wouldn't be such a headline. But this is Portia. Everything about her is always larger than life.

What makes it juicier is, supposedly, this new guy doesn't even go to our school. He's an *outsider*. The way people are talking about him, it's like he just landed his spaceship in the middle of the kickball game and said, "Take me to your leader." So they brought him to Portia. Obviously.

Think I caught a glimpse of him once at this frozen yogurt place Portia loves. Or maybe it wasn't him. That kid looked kind of familiar and everyone says the new guy is a stranger.

A lot of seventh-grade guys are bummed that Portia might be getting a boyfriend. Not me, though. No offense to her, but the less I think about Portia, the happier I'll be. Thinking about Portia always leads me to a pretty dark place.

If Portia had gotten a boyfriend a year ago, it's possible that a nobody like me never would have made the guest list for her birthday party. And while I might have been upset about it back then, I guarantee that my life would be a whole lot better today.

CHAPTER TWELVE

THEO METZINGER

Presenting the newest volunteer for Neighborhood Harvest Food Bank:

Me.

Not the Neighborhood Harvest branch near me. The one in Breezeway. Portia's branch.

I'm positive that Delgado Middle School holds the key to understanding what's happening to me. Otherwise, why would so many kids, including Portia, seem familiar when I've never been here before? Why would the area ring such a bell if it's a place I don't know? It's like I remember it, but I shouldn't. There's no way I've forgotten some kind of secret life, because then people would remember me too . . . and they don't. I have to figure out the connection, which means I have to keep coming back. And Portia is my excuse.

I usually meet her after school, which means I have to cut ninth period in order to bike to Breezeway in time. When I can't get away—like when I have a test or something—she goes straight to Neighborhood Harvest and I get there when I can. I've had to implement a couple of life hacks in order to make all this work. For example, I'm down to seeing Dr. Abagnale only once a week instead of twice, and in the evening instead of late afternoon. The same with karate—one class a week, on Saturday now. Dad gave me a hard time over that—the usual stuff about how soft I am—but it's actually working out okay. Biking back and forth to Breezeway is a lot more exercise than you get in any class.

On Wednesday, I arrive at Neighborhood Harvest around four thirty and find the warehouse in an uproar. Volunteers are scrambling all over the place, weighed down by armloads of heavy canned goods.

Portia provides the explanation. "Grab a carton and start loading! There are already forty people in line at Saint Basil's and more are coming every minute!"

For the next twenty minutes, Neighborhood Harvest is a madhouse. Packages of pasta and cereal sail through the air as the volunteers toss them our way to save time. Our hands are just a blur, stacking and stuffing. Portia leaps up and comes down with a cabbage in what would be a spectacular catch in any Major League Baseball stadium. It gets a big cheer, and she takes a quick bow. I try to make a similar play on a plastic bottle of pancake syrup, but it bounces off my fingers and skitters across the concrete floor. There are catcalls and a few boos, but nothing is allowed to interfere with the work we're doing. People are waiting for this food and it's our job to get it to them.

At last, the cartons are all full, and everyone is scrambling to load them onto the truck. It's so disorganized that Portia and I get stranded in the back of the payload, landlocked by the stacked boxes.

Dmitri, the supervisor, sees us trying to swim back out again and motions for us to sit down amid the cartons. "No time!" he calls. "Stay where you are. You can help with the distribution when you get to Saint Basil's."

That's how we end up riding to a Neighborhood Harvest food drive on the back of a truck, hemmed in by a hundred and fifty boxes of groceries.

Portia loves it. Pink-cheeked with pleasure, she hangs on to a pair of gallon milk jugs and giggles all the way. Even when a loaf of whole wheat bread rolls out of the top box and bounces off her head, it doesn't destroy the mood. That's Portia.

I grab it in midair and restore it to its proper box.

"You must be used to all this!" she calls over the engine's roar.

I'm mystified. "Why?"

"From when you worked on the trucks!"

Oops—I've got to watch that. When your life is built on lies, you'd better remember the details.

"Right!" I tell her. "But they didn't let us ride in the back. I'm pretty sure this is illegal!"

It only makes her laugh harder. "The cops would have to climb through all this to arrest us."

By now, I'm laughing too. It's a bumpy ride through the city streets, so I get a little seasick. But it's cool, because Portia's there. You can see why people are drawn to her. She has an enthusiasm for everything she does, and it's contagious. Bouncing around with the boxes, having your guts scrambled shouldn't be fun. But it is, thanks to her.

Portia bounces too, throwing out her arms to maintain a precarious balance. Watching her triggers another memory I've got no business having. Her arms are swaying, only she's not surrounded by boxes. She's dancing, a balloon in each hand. Holding back her long fair hair is a costume tiara, with the words HAPPY BIRTHDAY spelled out in sequins.

As she gyrates, one hand comes up to suppress a cough. In that instant, my happy recollection plummets into the depths of despair. Cold misery comes down on me like it's poured from the sky, and I'm trembling, even though I can't explain why.

When we get to Saint Basil's, I'm no use to anybody. While the others unload the truck, I'm in the churchyard, on my knees, dry-heaving into the bushes.

What is it about that memory that took me from having a good time and sank me to a place so awful that I'm physically sick? Portia dancing? What's so bad about that?

The bike ride home from Breezeway is always longer than the ride there. It's the same 4.6 miles. But by then, it's late rush hour, getting darker every day, and I'm sharing the road with more cars, who would like nothing better than to blast a cyclist into the ditch.

On Wednesdays, I skip dinner and go straight to Dr. Abagnale. She welcomes me the same as before, but with a look on her face like she smells something nasty. She probably does—me after all that pedaling.

By the time I make it home, I'm starving. Mom has a new line: "The kitchen is closed." I'm okay to make myself a peanut butter and jelly sandwich, but that's where the menu ends. She's trying to convince me to keep more regular hours, and I can't explain to her why that's not going to happen. These days, my gardening takes place in the dark, by flashlight, when you can't tell a weed from a vegetable, and it's barely possible to notice if Jaws has been snacking on my plants again. The green beans look a little nibbled, but I won't be sure until I see them in daylight.

My parents know that I'm volunteering at Neighborhood Harvest, but not that I'm doing it at the Breezeway branch on the south side. I don't tell anybody—especially not Dr. Abagnale—about Portia and why I have to spend so much time with her.

To be honest, if Portia went to my school, I don't think she'd ever choose to be friends with somebody like me. She's just too popular and out of my league. But at Delgado, I have a couple of advantages. First of all, I'm a stranger. Nobody knows me, so I *might* be cool. Second, and even more important, I have secret scouting on Portia via those memories that aren't mine but seem to be real. Like Neighborhood Harvest—I never could have hit it off with her in the first place if I didn't "remember" that she's a volunteer. When I said I was one too, that instantly gave us something big in common.

Example: I have a clear picture in my mind of her out in the neighborhood around Delgado walking a large German shepherd. So whenever we see a dog, I go into a long speech about what an animal lover I am, and how I'd take big dogs over little yappy ones any day. In another memory, she's mourning over a geometry quiz she flunked. So I've been brushing up on math, so I can help her with it. I have to do that anyway, since I have math in ninth period—the class I miss a lot in order to get to Portia.

If only I knew where these memories are coming from . . .

Even though I'm not telling anybody about my trips to Breezeway, I almost wish Dad could see me when I'm here. My life with the Delgado kids is a lot closer to the one he wants me to have than the one I'm actually living at home and my own school. I'm a man about town in Breezeway—at least, I go everywhere Portia does: Fro-Yo Joe's, Dunkin' Donuts, the bookshop, the convenience store. I even have a nickname among some of the guys. They call me Basket Case because of the basket on my bike. The old Theo would probably take that personally, but here, it's kind of my trademark. I don't have a trademark in my real life.

When you hang out with the most popular girl in school, some of the popularity rubs off on you. Also, I'm not shy here. I can't afford to be. If Portia gets bored with me, there goes my only lead to understanding what's happening to me.

I always assumed I was shy because it was in my DNA or something. Who would have thought it was something I could change like my underwear?

I've got serious reasons for coming to Breezeway, but I have to admit it's fun to play at being someone you're not. And if I blow it here, I can always go back to being the real me.

One afternoon, Portia shows up at Fro-Yo Joe's with a scrape on her cheek. "Kickball injury," she explains, half sheepish, half proud. "I slid into second on my face. Safe."

"High-stakes game," I comment.

"The highest—bragging rights. The whole seventh grade is in on it." She rattles off a list of names, most of them the kids who've dubbed me Basket Case. "And Reef," she finishes, turning suddenly melancholy. "He used to play. You know . . . *before*."

Reef. It's an unusual name, but for some reason, it rings a bell with me.

"Who's Reef?" I ask.

Portia's eyes grow shadowed. "It's the saddest story you ever heard. This kid—his mom died of Covid last year. She was so nice. She worked at the bank over on Willow Street."

The memory slams into my head like a blow from a sledgehammer. I *know* that bank! I stood across the street and *remembered* a lady sitting in that glassed-in office! The sight of her almost made me cry! Was that the same mom . . . the one who died?

Portia is still talking about this kid Reef. "He had no dad, no grandparents, no family. His mother's friend took him in, so he's got a place to live. But you can tell he's totally miserable."

"I want to meet him!" I blurt.

Both her eyebrows go up. "That's not such a good idea. We used to be friends. He even came to my birthday party. But after it happened, he shut everybody out. Not that I'm blaming him. What the poor guy's been through—it's unbelievable!"

I can't let the subject drop. I've been so positive that Portia is the connection to the answers I've been searching for. Could it be this kid Reef?

"Maybe he's weird around you guys because you knew him when his whole life fell apart," I reason. "I'm new here. He might talk to me even if he can't open up to you."

"I guess." She doesn't sound convinced. "He doesn't like me very much anymore. Whenever he sees me, he heads in the opposite direction." It really seems to bother her. When you're Portia and everybody flocks to you, it's hard to understand rejection.

"I'll come early tomorrow," I promise. "Meet me in front of the school and you can point him out as he leaves."

A frown creases that perfect forehead. She's probably wondering why I'm suddenly so obsessed with this one kid. I can't explain it to her; I can barely explain it to myself. But I feel like I'm close. I can't let this get away from me.

"Okay," she finally agrees.

I spend the whole next day in a state of anxiety.

"Someone's excited this morning," Mom observes at breakfast.

"No, it's just another day!" Even my voice is squeaky. "Why excited? What makes you think I'm excited?"

Kristi laughs in my face. "Well, for one thing, you got more cereal on the place mat than in your mouth."

Even Jaws seems to catch an aura off me. As I start down the front walk, he backs out of the flower bed and watches me with his head tilted quizzically to the side, as if he too notices something different about me today.

"I'm *not* excited!" I throw him a dirty look as I head to the garage to get my bike.

Halfway through eighth period, I sneak out of school. I can't take the chance that I might not get to Delgado in time to meet up with Portia and intercept Reef at dismissal.

Wouldn't you know it—there's construction on the Thirteenth Street Bridge, and I have to go around the long way. When I have a near miss with a cement truck, my first thought is not *I almost got killed*. It's *What if I'm late today of all days?* That's how wound up I am.

Delgado's distant bell sounds just as I wheel around the corner and the white cupola comes into view. I raise myself off the seat, putting my full weight into pedaling the last block. I stash my bike and sprint for the front steps.

There's an art to middle school dismissal. Never stand right in front of the exit unless you want to get trampled—especially if the eighth graders come out first. The smart move is to back off and let the initial stampede pass.

True to her word, Portia is one of the first ones out of the building.

"Did I miss him?" I ask anxiously.

She shakes her head. "The seventh-grade wing is toward the back. He's not out yet."

The flow of people is like striking oil—a gusher at first, but eventually, it slows to a trickle. Portia stands beside me, scanning the emerging faces.

"That's him."

She doesn't need to say it. When Reef appears, I know exactly who he is. He's the kid I saw that first day peering in the window of Fro-Yo Joe's—the one from my memory of looking in the mirror.

No wonder Portia thinks of him as "that poor kid." Even from a distance, you can see that he's suffering. There's a grimness to him, a tension. His shoulders are being held too high, like he can't relax. A thin line surrounds his mouth, indicating that his jaw is clenched. The kids around him are socializing, laughing, chattering, but he doesn't seem to notice any of it. He talks to nobody, his eyes downcast.

Maybe I recognize him so easily because I've *felt* that sadness—*his* sadness. In a dizzying rush, I return to my vision of the sick woman in the hospital bed. His mother? Yeah—I have no trouble believing that's the kind of devastation you feel when someone you love is dying.

Which still doesn't explain why *I* would experience *his* memories.

"Reef—" Portia begins tentatively.

His response, almost automatic, is "Oh, hi. Gotta run—"

But he doesn't run—and not because of Portia either. He freezes when he catches sight of me.

"I'm Theo," I say aloud.

"I—I know."

He *recognizes* me—just like I recognize him!

What's going on?

CHAPTER THIRTEEN

REEF MOODY

This can't be happening!

I must have thought that to myself a hundred times when Mom was sick. But this is the first time the thought is racing through my head because I'm looking at something absolutely, positively, one hundred percent *impossible.*

This kid—Theo—the one they call Basket Case—I've seen him before. And not just hanging around Portia. He's in my memories. But here's where it goes off the chain: I don't *remember* him so much as . . . I *am* him.

All that gardening I know I've never done—every now and then I'll catch a glimpse of my reflection in a window. It should be my face, but it isn't.

Fact is, I'm looking at that face right now.

Portia sticks herself into the odd standoff between the two of us. "You guys *know* each other?"

"No," we reply at the same time. Then, also at the same time, "I mean—" We both fall silent again.

"This is weird," Portia concludes, studying our expressions. "You get that you're acting weird, right?"

Weird isn't the half of it! How often do you run into a face you remember from your own reflection?

I take a flying leap. "Is there any chance that you have . . . a rabbit?"

Theo seems astounded. "You know Jaws?"

I think of those gigantic square teeth sticking out of that tiny furry face, and a short laugh is torn from my throat. "Jaws—right!"

"We have to talk," Theo says urgently.

"Definitely," I agree.

And we're actually starting to walk away when we realize that Portia is still standing there, staring at us.

"Catch you later?" Theo offers, looking torn. Maybe he thinks he's putting his potential boyfriend status at risk.

"Don't worry about me," she says sarcastically. "I love being ignored."

But it doesn't take long for her to fall in with a group heading to Fro-Yo Joe's. That leaves me alone with Basket Case. We wander to a picnic table on the school grounds and sit down, facing one another.

"Listen," I tell him. "Why are you here? I mean—I think I know. But I need to hear it from you first."

Theo pauses for a long time. I think he's planning out what he's going to say. Believe me, I can relate. If he's going through anything like what I am, finding the right words to describe it could take years.

At last, he begins, "There are things I remember that I know for a fact never happened to me."

"Me too!" I jump in breathlessly.

"But it's more than just my mind playing tricks," Theo

goes on. "The memories feel real. They're just not mine. Are they yours?"

I'm surprised, but a split second later, I realize I shouldn't be. My own "fake" memories—they're not random images that somehow found their way into my head. They're from the real life of another person—a kid who likes gardening, and goes to a karate class, and knows a rabbit named Jaws. A kid whose mom took him to the penguin exhibit when he was a little kid. A kid named Theo.

"You're the gardener, right?" I ask. "And that's your dad who's always pushing you to be tougher?"

He looks embarrassed. "He's not a bad guy. He wants what's best for me. But it has to be what *he* thinks is best."

"Because"—a phrase pops into my head—"he ruled the school."

Theo looks shocked for a moment and then breaks into a nervous laugh. "You really are the right guy. Makes sense, I guess. If I've got your memories, why shouldn't you have mine?"

"Is this, like, a *disease*?" I wonder. "We both got sick, and now our brains are . . . switching heads?"

"Not our brains. I'm still me and you're still you. But I *remember* your life like I'm the guy who lived it. And vice versa."

"And it's happening because . . . ?"

Theo shakes his head. "No clue. But we're not wrong about this. We're not imagining it, we're not hallucinating, and we're not confused. When I tried to explain what I was seeing to my mom, she sent me to a psychiatrist!"

"I should be grateful I don't talk to anybody at home," I put in.

"The point is," he goes on, "we have to back each other up, because we're the only ones who can. Anybody else we try to tell will think we're either lying or totally bananas."

I wish he wasn't right, but I already know he is. I picture myself trying to explain this to Willis or Jenna. They'd figure that I lost my mind, collapsing under all the stress after Mom died. If a kid with two parents got sent to see a shrink, I wonder what would happen to somebody like me. Whatever it is, Declan would enjoy it, that's for sure. He'd probably set up a chair on the lawn so he could watch me being taken away by the guys in the white coats.

I lean back on the wooden bench and sigh. "So what happens now? We both agree this is real. What do we do about it?"

His face falls. "I never thought about it beyond finding you. I have no idea what comes next."

Disappointment washes over me. So there it is. Not that I thought we could press a magic button and all this would be fixed. But when Theo tracked me down out of an entire city, sue me for hoping he'd have more to offer than "I have no idea."

"I was afraid you'd say something like that. Come to think of it, how *did* you find me? There must be thousands of kids just like me in this town."

"I used your memories. First the school." He points. "That cupola. And when I came here to check it out, I knew Portia because *you* did. So I made friends with her, figuring she could lead me to you."

Have to smile at that. "A lot of guys in this school would be really relieved to know that. They think you're hitting on the most popular girl at Delgado." My grin fades in a hurry. If Theo recognized Portia from my memories—well, my memories of Portia tell the story of the worst thing that ever happened in my life.

I fold my arms over my chest. "So you have my memories. Like what?"

He looks away from me. "I know you've had a rough time. I know you lost your mom and I know you don't love the place where you're living. I know you share a room with a guy who treats you pretty rotten . . ."

My jaw is stiffening. What other memories has Basket Case been eavesdropping on? Maybe the one where I got Covid at Portia's party and passed it on to my mother. Does this *stranger* know how Mom would still be alive if I hadn't been such a jerk about that one stupid thing?

Theo is still speaking. "I know it was just you and your mom and the two of you were really close. I know she worked in that bank near the school. I know she must have been a great mom, because she had a special smile just for looking at you."

My temper rises up the back of my throat. I don't even remember that smile, and *he* does?

It hits me: If Theo has access to my memories, how can he remember what I can't? The answer is so obvious: He's not *sharing* my memories; he's *stealing* them. The reason I can't call up an image of my mother is because he's taken them away!

I leap to my feet. "You remember my mother's smile, huh? Did you ever think about how that works?" He gives me a blank look. "When you remember that smile, you claim it for yourself. So I hope you're satisfied, because I can't see it anymore!"

Theo is horrified. "I didn't know! I mean—why would that happen? Am I losing *my* memories to *you*?"

"What do you care?" I snap, my tone bitter. "If you forget your petunias, you can plant new ones—" I deliberately cut myself off. I was about to say *But you only get one mother!* I don't think I could have made it through that without my voice cracking.

He stands up too. "I'm not doing anything! Not on purpose! The memories just come to me! Honest!"

He looks sincere and I believe him. He isn't doing any of this intentionally. But that doesn't change the fact that it's happening.

I couldn't care less that this isn't his fault. I'm losing my mother, and he's the reason why. Just the thought that he's able to see her and I'm not gnaws at me like a flesh-eating infection. I can't stand it, not for another second.

"Stay away from me!" I almost spit the words at him. "And stay out of my head!"

He spreads his arms wide. "I don't know if I can."

"Try harder!"

I stalk away, my furious footsteps pounding divots into the lawn.

“If you change your mind,” he calls after me, “Portia has my number.”

Well, that makes it easy. It’s already my life’s purpose to keep my distance from Portia. How hard can it be to make sure I never see this Theo kid again?

CHAPTER FOURTEEN

THEO METZINGER

In perfect unison, fourteen fists strike out at imaginary opponents. The Seidokwan dojo echoes with our *kiai*—the shouts that add focus and strength to our attacking moves.

Sensei casts me an approving nod. He's noticed that I'm putting a lot of effort into today's class. He probably thinks he's finally reached me. In reality, this is less about martial arts and more about Reef.

If I'm stealing his memories of his mother, then I have to do everything I can to stop it. The last thing I want is to add to that poor kid's misery.

The problem is, I don't know what I'm doing to grab those memories away from him. It just happens. I reach back into my mind and the whole thing is already there, like I'm the person it happened to. Only it didn't happen to me; it happened to *him*.

If I can't prevent myself from remembering, the one thing I can do is keep my mind busy, so it doesn't have time to wander into Reef territory. Karate is great for that, because it's all about focusing and concentrating and meditating. And whenever Reef's mom starts to pop into my head, I leap right into some jumping jacks or drop down for some push-ups—anything to change the focus and clear my mind. I hope it's working. The only way to know for sure would be to ask Reef. And that's not an option. The guy hates my guts, and I can't even blame him.

Toward the end of class, we're partnered up and sparring when Adele Pulaski's foot slams into the side of my head so hard that I see stars.

Sitting flat on my butt on the mat, I look up at her. "What did you do that for?"

She's mystified. "Why didn't you block it?"

"I didn't know it was coming!"

"We've been working on the reverse crescent kick for two weeks!" she insists.

"What are you talking about? I don't know any reverse crescent—" But even as I'm saying it, I have to admit it sounds kind of familiar.

I look around the dojo. The other six sparring pairs are taking turns practicing the very same kick Adele used to deck me. Some are pretty good; some are awkward and clumsy. But everybody seems to know what's coming and how to block it. Everybody but me.

Okay, I'm not exactly the star of the class. But how could I forget a kick we've been working on for two weeks? Unless I remember it just fine and the memory went to Reef. That would mean this memory-stealing business works both ways.

Reef knows exactly what he's losing, because forgetting your poor dead mom is so devastating. But how am I ever going to be able to keep track of what's missing from my mind? How much else is gone? And how do I find out? Except like this—the hard way.

For example, yesterday I went out to the garden to pick my strawberries and they were all gone. It had to be Jaws. Some gratitude—I saved him from Dad, and this is the thanks I get. But then Mom dragged me into the kitchen and opened the refrigerator.

There was the bowl brimming with strawberries that I picked just yesterday.

Does Reef have a memory of that?

I sure don't.

Memory: the mental process of registering, storing, and retrieving information.

I find a few different definitions of memory on the internet, but they all say the same thing: Your brain acts pretty much the way a computer does. A computer stores information in electronic bits. The human brain uses something similar—a combination of electrical and chemical signals. Nerve cells work together in patterns called synapses. So when you remember something, your brain just triggers these synapses to call what's stored there back up.

Presto: memory.

Simple. Well, not really. Picture the most complicated science class you ever didn't understand and multiply it by fifty. There are whole maps of different regions of the brain with names like *cerebral cortex* and *hippocampus*, which sounds like the college hippopotamuses go to. Or is that hippopotami?

It's pretty confusing. On one website, I read that there are three types of memory. But in other places, they talk about five types of memory and even seven. So what are you supposed to believe?

Three types—that's what makes the most sense to me. Those are short term, long term, and sensory. Short term has nothing to do with what's happening between Reef and me. Your short-term memory is *really* short term—what happened in the last thirty seconds. There's no way we're swapping memories that quickly. If that was true, we'd lose track of stuff while it's still going on, like sitting in a chair and forgetting what you're doing before your butt hits the seat.

A karate kick, or picking berries—even if those things happened only yesterday—count as long-term memory. Also Reef remembering his mom—although some of those memories could be sensory, the third kind. The sound of her voice, the smell of her shampoo, or the feeling of her holding his hand when he was little—all that would be sensory memory.

We're trading long-term and sensory memories. It's affecting both of us, but it's tougher on Reef because of his mom. His memories are all he has left of her, and there's a limit to them. No wonder he's emotional about this. When *they're* gone, *she's* gone.

I close the lid of my laptop and slump in my chair, exhausted. I can read about this stuff until the cows come home, but I'll never get what I'm looking for. Whole libraries have been written about how memories get imprinted in your brain, mountains of books on subjects like how you remember, what you remember, why you remember, and even why you forget. But there's not a single word about two seventh graders whose memories are bouncing back and forth between them like Ping-Pong balls. And there can only be one explanation for that: What's happening with Reef and me isn't supposed to be happening. I can google it for years instead of hours and I won't be any closer to an answer.

It's going to take the two of us together to figure this out . . . if it can be done at all. And he won't even talk to me.

The doorbell rings, and a moment later, my mom calls up to me. "Theo! Your friend is here."

Friend? I check my phone. I'm not expecting anyone, and there are no texts telling me somebody's on the way over. To be honest, I'm not the most social guy in the world. As Dad puts it, my BFFs are carrots. It's not that I don't have friends, but they tend to be kids I chill with at school. Who's here now?

I go to the top of the stairs and look down into the front hall.

There, standing just inside the door, is Reef.

What's he doing here? This doesn't look very much like *Stay away from me and stay out of my head!*

I almost wipe out twice getting down the stairs.

My mother looks pleased. I don't get a lot of visitors. "Don't keep your friend waiting," she whispers.

Reef is listening to Kristi, who is jabbering at the speed of light. I may suffer from shyness, but my sister is my polar opposite.

I open the door and usher Reef outside. Kristi moves to follow, but Mom holds her back.

I sit down on the porch swing and Reef leans against the wrought iron rail opposite me.

I ask the first question that pops into my head. "How did you find me?"

He grimaces, like talking about it causes him pain. "I remember your street."

It makes no sense to anybody but me. I must have looked at the sign that says Forest Avenue five thousand times. If a few of those memories went to Reef, I'd never miss them. But he'd have the name to type into Google Maps.

"It took me three buses to get here," he goes on in amazement. "But once I was in the neighborhood, it was like my feet knew exactly where to go."

I nod. "That's the way it works. When I first got to Breezeway, everything looked familiar." An awkward silence falls between us, so I add, "Why did you come?"

"I have to ask you something," he says earnestly. "Something maybe only you can answer."

"Okay."

"Am I a thief?"

Of all the questions I'm expecting, this has to be last on the list.

"Of course not! I mean, I don't think so. I mean—what are we really talking about here?"

"My principal's pocketbook was stolen out of her office at

school," he explains uncomfortably. "And I got blamed for it. The thing is, I've never stolen anything in my life and I don't remember stealing this. But after the other day, when we talked about how things are, I thought maybe I'm guilty after all. And the reason I don't remember is that the memory went to you."

I close my eyes, conjuring up the image of a lady's purse to use like a search keyword as I sift through my memory. If Reef did this, one of the two of us has to remember it.

"I've got nothing," I confess. "That's good news, right? It means you're innocent."

He shakes his head sadly. "The pocketbook turned up in my sock drawer, minus the money. So I still look guilty."

And just like that, it comes to me, almost out of nowhere. I'm in bed, half asleep, but it isn't my room; it's the bedroom where that other kid threw the geode. And there he is, tiptoeing across the floor. It's really dark and I'm barely conscious, but . . . what's that in his hand? I catch a glimpse of it in the gloom: a leather pocketbook.

The kid eases open the top dresser drawer, drops the purse inside, and silently shuts the drawer again.

"Your roommate," I begin.

He leans forward. "Declan. What about him?"

"I remember—*you* remember Declan sneaking across the room in the middle of the night and hiding the pocketbook in your dresser." I pause, breathless. "You didn't steal that purse; *he* did. And he planted it in your drawer."

Reef pales. "Yeah, that's what I figured. Or maybe I didn't. These days I'm so mixed up, anything's possible."

"What are you going to do?" I ask.

He shrugs miserably. "Nothing. Who'll back me up?"

"I will," I volunteer.

"Yeah, but how are you going to explain how you know?"

A protest rises up in my throat. Reef can't let people go on believing that he's a thief! And Declan shouldn't be allowed to get away with framing him! But the more I think about it, the more I realize the poor kid has no choice. Even if he tells the truth as he knows it now, how's he going to explain why he waited so long before defending himself? He's stuck between a rock and a hard place. He's got no choice but to go on living with the jerk who treats him like garbage and a family who considers him a crook. I feel really bad for him. My life may not be perfect, but I've never been stuck in a lose-lose situation like that.

Reef gets oddly formal. "Okay. Thank you very much."

"Hey," I say suddenly, "I know this isn't as important as your thing, but I've got a question for you. You wouldn't happen to remember picking a bowl of strawberries a couple of days ago, would you?"

A half smile appears on his face. "You didn't want to let them get too ripe. Whatever that means." He stands up. "Must be nice, having nothing bigger to worry about than picking fruit."

It stings, but I have to admit he has a point.

"Listen, man," I tell him. "I know you've got more problems than I do. But our biggest problem is exactly the same. This thing with our memories isn't going away. Maybe if we put our heads together, we can figure out what's happening to us."

He seems unimpressed. "I've got three buses to catch. It's a long way back to Breezeway. I don't know how you stand it. You must really like Portia."

"I bike it," I tell him.

"I don't have a bike. I could borrow Declan's, except he wouldn't give me the skin off a grape." He starts down the porch stairs but freezes on the bottom step.

Jaws is sitting on the front walk, staring up at Reef in—what? Terror? Fascination?

Reef squats down and runs his fingers through the wild rabbit's silky ears. "How's it going, Jaws?"

Out of sheer habit, I stomp on the floorboards of the porch, and Jaws darts away, his brown fur just a blur.

Reef casts me a disgusted look and starts off down the sidewalk.

CHAPTER FIFTEEN

REEF MOODY

I'm starting to think I hate everybody.

Okay, maybe *hate* is a strong word, but how else do I describe the way I feel about the people in my life right now? Like Jenna and Principal Latimore, who've got me doing chores to pay back money that I didn't even steal. Or Willis, who signed off on it. Or Liam and Carolyn, who act like I barely even exist. Same goes for my so-called friends—all the kids at school who drop their gaze and look the other way, because they don't dare look me in the eye.

Even Basket Case Theo, who thinks we now have to be blood brothers because of the weird connection between our minds. I don't blame him for what's happening to us. I doubt he has any more choice about it than I do. But he's taking away all my memories of my mother. His fault or not, I can't ever forgive him for that.

Then there's Declan. I save him for last because he's the worst. I don't blame him for considering me a charity case who invaded his house and his room—no disagreement with that. But now that I know for sure about Latimore's pocketbook, my opinion of that guy has blasted through the subbasement down to the Earth's core. I thought you couldn't get any lower than a liar and a bully and a thief. Guess not.

I can't start anything at home, where I'm outnumbered. But the very next day, I catch up with Declan on the way to school.

"I know," I tell him darkly.

He snorts. "What is it you think you know?"

"That you're the one who stole Latimore's pocketbook. And I know you took the money and stashed the purse in my sock drawer."

He doesn't try to deny it. Laughs like he's just heard the most hilarious joke in history.

"So what are you going to do about it?" I demand.

He shrugs. "If you think I'm going to own up, Reek, dream on."

"Yeah, well, I can tell Willis and Jenna what I know."

"You mean *my* parents, who aren't related to you at all?" he sneers.

The fury wells up inside me until I picture myself as a blowfish at full inflation, huge and round. If I can't get justice, I want revenge, and three words come to me from a place in my mind I can't quite identify: *reverse crescent kick*. Even though I can't place it, I *remember* it. My body knows how to do it. The blanks quickly fill themselves in: a karate dojo; the sensei who taught it to me; the fluid motion of the leg as it rises toward the target. It's going to feel great to put Declan on the sidewalk.

Just as I'm enjoying the anticipation of knocking Declan into next Thursday, I realize that I don't dare. If I can get myself into this much trouble over something I *didn't* do, imagine what would happen if I clobbered this jerk. Fact is, we're right by Delgado. The sidewalks are full—parents dropping off their kids; buses unloading. Hundreds of witnesses.

And anyway, it just feels wrong. Not attacking Declan—no one's ever deserved it more. But that karate kick is Theo's, not mine. Using it would be taking advantage of our strange connection. I don't want any part of that. For all I know, it might even strengthen the highway between our heads.

Hard pass on that.

All day at school, whenever I see Declan in the halls, he beams at me. It's more than his usual nasty scowl. It says that I know the worst thing he ever did, but I'm so worthless and weak that he has nothing to fear from me.

I do see Declan once without the smile that day. I'm on my way home when I spot him at the entrance to an alley, deep in conversation with a kid I can't place at first. He's taller, older, definitely not a Delgado student. Then I remember why. He was expelled last year. There are plenty of rumors why, but the big picture seems to be that he was the middle school equivalent of a criminal.

It takes a lot to get suspended in our school. It didn't happen to me when they believed I robbed the principal herself. So I can only imagine what you have to do get kicked out forever, like—

The name comes to me: Konrad Sikorsky.

Why is Declan hanging around with *him*? Maybe bad people attract each other like magnets.

But Declan, awful as he is, isn't Sikorsky bad. Konrad is the kind of kid who's going to be in jail one day. Everybody calls him Konvict—but never to his face. You don't want to come to his attention for any reason at all. No question about it. Declan is asking for big trouble just breathing the same air as him.

Then I say to myself: What do I care? Was I put on this Earth to be Declan's guardian angel? He's been treating me like snail slime since the day Jenna brought me home with her. If Declan wants to ruin his life—well, it couldn't happen to a nicer guy.

The thought of Jenna stops me in my tracks. I'm not thrilled with my living setup, but she's practically a saint. I've known her since I was first old enough to open my eyes. Some of my earliest memories are hearing her and my mother giggling like third graders—I still have some ear memories, at least. She was a loyal best friend to Mom and never deserted her. Even after Mom was gone, she took me in when I had no place else to go.

If Declan gets mixed up with Konrad, he could wind up in jail, or maybe even get himself killed. I don't care about Declan, but I can't let that happen to Declan's mother.

Jenna works an early shift, so she's always home by the time I get back from school. She's got one of her famous banana breads under construction when I pull her aside in the kitchen. One thing about the Helmer house—the cooking smells are world class.

"I need to talk to you. It's Declan—I just saw him—"

She raises an oven-mitted hand like a cop stopping traffic. "I'm not blind, Reef. I know you and Declan don't get along. I hope that improves as you grow older. But I can't let myself be dragged into your disputes."

"This isn't a dispute," I insist. "I saw him with Konrad Sikorsky. Do you know who that is?"

"My kids—and that includes you—associate with whoever they choose. Yes, I know—Declan got himself into some trouble. So did you, by the way."

"This is *different*," I plead. "This is something to be worried about."

She loads the loaf pan into the oven. "You're working to pay back what you owe the principal. And I'm hoping Declan's community service will have a positive effect on him too. He starts next week at Neighborhood Harvest Food Bank."

Neighborhood Harvest . . . why does that sound familiar?

CHAPTER SIXTEEN

THEO METZINGER

I'm on my bike, three-quarters of the way to Breezeway, when my phone pings.

I pull over to the side of the road and check the incoming text. It's from Portia: *Can't make it to NH today. Have to visit my aunt. Tell Dmitri sorry.*

I groan aloud. She could have saved me a lot of pedaling—and a skipped math class—if this text had come an hour ago.

It isn't her fault—she doesn't know how far away I live. How can I tell her that without having to explain all of it?

I text back: *Np. I'll explain to Dmitri.* I don't allow myself to think about how much less fun it's going to be to stack shelves, pack boxes, and load trucks without Portia.

When I get to the warehouse, I find Dmitri, the supervisor, and explain that it's going to be just me today.

"Glad you're here, Theo. We're understaffed. Plus," he adds, lowering his voice, "you can keep an eye on the new guy."

"New guy?"

The supervisor inclines his head in the direction of a tall, rangy kid, maybe a little older than me. He's perched on a chair that has one short leg, and he's rocking back and forth on it in an obnoxious way that makes you wish the whole thing would tip over and spill him out on his head.

I'm just reflecting that he looks strangely familiar when Dmitri calls, "Hey, Declan, quit clowning around and unload that shipment of clam chowder."

Declan! It comes to me in a rush of memories—not mine, Reef's! This is the guy Reef lives with! The one who threw a geode at him and framed him for stealing the principal's pocketbook! Surely he's the last person in the world who would donate his time to work for a worthy cause like Neighborhood Harvest.

"*He* volunteers here?"

"More like he was volun-*told*," Dmitri replies. "The cops volunteered him. Community service."

That sounds more like Declan. Anyone who could steal his principal's pocketbook and frame his own roommate for it definitely does plenty of other things you get sentenced to community service for.

"Listen, Dmitri," I whisper, "I know this kid. He's bad news. I don't think we can trust him."

The supervisor shrugs. "What can he steal? Clam chowder? I hate clam chowder." Then he adds, "But watch him around the locker room. People put stuff there."

So while I'm working, I try to keep track of Declan. As far as I can see, he isn't doing anything wrong. He isn't doing anything, period. The guy has elevated goofing off to the level of high art. The closest he comes to stealing happens when he hijacks a can of Chef Boyardee. In a corner, he perches on a stepladder and eats cold ravioli with his fingers.

"That's not for snacking, Helmer," Dmitri growls at him. "People rely on this food."

Declan's reply is a satisfied belch.

My heart aches for Reef, who I don't even like. He has to live with this slob, who spends more time in the bathroom than the warehouse. And considering that the bathroom is located off the locker room . . .

I venture back there during one bathroom break, and see Declan fiddling with locks. I clear my throat loudly.

He's startled but insists on walking around, acting casual. "What are you looking at, kid?"

"Nothing," I say. But I don't leave the locker room until he does.

At the end of the day, Dmitri signs Declan's community service form, which is a lot more than the guy deserves.

I'm getting on my bike, not relishing the thought of the long ride back to my side of town, when I see Declan slouching down the street. It dawns on me: He's going home to where Reef lives. If I follow him, I'll know where to find Reef.

Declan would make a lousy CIA agent. He doesn't notice me behind him, biking in circles so I don't zoom past him. Pretty soon, though, I know exactly where I'm going. I've experienced it many times before, through Reef's memories. I see the street before Declan turns onto it. I even recognize the house—the third from the dead end on the left-hand side.

He disappears inside and I stop on the other side of the

road, repeating the address to myself: 44 Poplar Drive. I take out my phone and type it into the notes, since these days, information doesn't always stay with me very long. That makes me snicker—the notion that Reef might experience a recollection of sitting on a bike across from his own house, memorizing his address, which he already knows.

I'm about to ride away when a voice calls "Hey!" and a few seconds later, Reef is standing by my handlebars, holding on to my bike by the basket. "Are you spying on me? How did you find where I live?"

I tell him the truth. "I followed Declan. He was at the food bank where I volunteer. I recognized him from your memories."

"What do you want with Declan?"

"You were right about him. He's a jerk." I feel my face flush. "Okay, I *was* spying. But only because I want to be able to find you if I need you."

That makes him mad. "You don't need me, and I don't need you. We're totally separate people, and let's keep it that way."

"We can't keep it that way, and you know it," I counter. "You thought maybe you did steal that pocketbook until I told you that you didn't. And there are things that I can't know without you."

"Oh, sure," he scoffs. "Name one."

"Well, for starters—have I ever been to Florida?"

He looks surprised. "What are you talking about?"

"Last night, my sister brought out her photo album of our trip to Disney World. I'm in all the pictures. But if I had to swear on a Bible, I would say I was never there."

Reef puts his head down, thinks it over, and comes up smiling. "Sure, you were there. You threw up on Space Mountain. And again on Pirates of the Caribbean."

My face is definitely getting even redder. "So long as I had a good time."

"You had a great time," he insists. "You celebrated your birthday in the hotel and your grandparents drove up from Fort Lauderdale."

There's something really annoying about having the time of your life but not remembering one nanosecond of it. "Must have been spring break," I reflect. "March twenty-third is my birthday."

He gets a strange look on his face. "March twenty-third? That's your birthday?"

I nod.

"Me too!"

I frown. "That's a pretty big coincidence."

"Or maybe it isn't a coincidence at all."

We stare at each other. Reef and I are connected by a phenomenon that, as far as we know, has never happened to anybody else in the history of the world. And now we learn we were both born on exactly the same day, maybe even the same moment. That has to be important.

"It *sounds* big," I say slowly, "but I guess we really don't know anything yet. There must be millions of other kids born on that day, but we're not getting *their* memories."

"Maybe we're the closest two," he muses.

"There has to be more to it than that . . ." I shake my head to clear it. "It doesn't make sense! You shouldn't remember my trip to Florida, and I shouldn't remember your—" I stop myself just in time. Any time I mention Reef's mother, our conversation usually goes down the drain fast.

This time, though, Reef is hooked. Our shared birthday may not prove anything, but it shows us that there's a way to investigate what's happening to us. Get to know each other. Find things we have in common. Those are the places to look for clues.

We exchange numbers. "Call me anytime," I urge. "Nothing is as important as getting to the bottom of this."

He nods. "I will. And take care of my memories. I want them back."

I know exactly which memories he's talking about.

CHAPTER SEVENTEEN

REEF MOODY

Just because I gave Theo my number doesn't mean I like the guy. We're just stuck together, that's all.

Fact is, we need each other. He's right about that. The thing about our birthday—we never could have learned that except by talking it out. We have to keep talking, because you never know what little fact might help us understand what's going on. *The Phenomenon*, Theo calls it. That's the perfect word for it, since it has no explanation. On top of everything else that's happened in the last year, I'm sharing a phenomenon with a guy called Basket Case.

The annoying part? Let's start with his texts. When I agreed to stay in touch, I didn't think that meant twenty times a day. I'll be sitting in math class when I feel a vibration coming from my pocket. So I risk big trouble to check my messages under the desk—remember, I'm still on probation at school.

And there it is. From Theo: *Did I ever break my arm?*

I sift through the memories I have from him and type back: *Rollerblading accident, fourth grade.*

I don't fill in the details, like he must have been the biggest chicken ever to strap on a pair of Rollerblades. I remember the sheer terror of picking up speed down a hill. The kid deliberately threw himself into a parked car, because something had to stop him. And I can see Dad—*Theo's* dad, who bought him blades so he could play roller hockey—paying the owner of the car for his busted window. There's more: The pain of the fracture wasn't half as bad as how itchy it got once the cast had been on for a few weeks. A knitting needle, jammed under the plaster, was the only thing that helped.

I smile a little. Serves him right.

No sooner is the phone back in my pocket than it's buzzing again.

Any idea where I put my library card?

I've already thumbed *Bug off!* when it comes to me—Theo in the lunchroom using the laminated card to dislodge a piece of chicken nugget that got stuck between his front teeth. That's another thing about the Phenomenon: You get the gross memories too. He rinsed the card off in the drinking fountain and stuck it in the small compartment in his backpack. Mystery solved.

By the way, Theo never asks about memories that involve Portia, although I've picked up a bunch of those too. He claims that he only hung out with Portia to find his way to me, but I know he's got a crush on her. You can't lie to someone who's in your head. Sooner or later, everybody has a crush on Portia. Me too.

And look where it got me.

When I meet the Metzingers, it's hard to pretend it's for the first time. I already know them well, courtesy of the Phenomenon.

It's hard to figure out Theo's dad. The nice guy who invites me into his house doesn't really match the father in Theo's memories. Every word he says triggers a cascade of arguments between him and Theo over the years. And while they don't bother me, I can tell that they bothered Theo plenty when they were going on.

"Your dad's nicer than I expected," I tell Theo when we go out to the backyard. "Not the type to spend a hundred and fifty bucks on a rabbit trap."

He looks startled. "Wai—what rabbit trap?"

I shrug. "If I've got the memory, you might have lost it."

His reply is a nervous laugh. "It makes sense. We went to war with Jaws a few weeks ago. Jaws won."

He gives me a tour of the vegetable garden, which I've already seen a hundred times in my mind. I even identify a couple of grubs that might pose a danger to the leafy stuff. Thanks to the Phenomenon, I'm a regular Farmer Brown.

Mr. Metzinger lights the barbecue and gives us a long lecture about how grilling with mesquite gives meat the most flavor. It's my first glimpse of what Theo sees in his dad. There are two ways of doing everything in the world: his way and the wrong way. And if you ever fail to live up to his standards, you're letting him down.

While the burgers and chicken are cooking, Theo's kid sister, Kristi, drags me inside by the arm to show me all her sports trophies on the mantel over the fireplace. She's a real chatterbox, and she keeps an iron grip on my wrist as she babbles on about every goal she ever scored, every homer she ever hit, and every basket she ever sank.

Mrs. Metzinger bails me out. "Dinner's ready."

We eat at the picnic table on the patio. "This is really good," I compliment Theo's dad, who did all the cooking.

I get the mesquite lecture again. Theo shoots me a meaningful look that plainly says: *Don't give him a chance to educate us one more time.* Sorry, Basket Case. I just might. Kind of enjoying watching you suffer.

I'm halfway through my burger when Kristi exclaims, "Look!"

We all follow her pointing finger. Jaws is in the grass just a few feet away, approaching the picnic table cautiously but steadily.

"I can't believe he isn't afraid of us," Mrs. Metzinger comments.

"Blame Theo," her husband complains. "I tried to get rid of him. Your son wouldn't let me."

"That's not it," Kristi half whispers. "It's because he can tell Reef's a good person."

No question about it: The rabbit's eyes are locked on me.

Theo rolls his eyes. "Come on, Kristi. You don't seriously believe that a rabbit can tell who's naughty and who's nice. That's Santa Claus, not the Easter Bunny."

"Animals like me," I offer. "We always had pets. You know, before . . ." My voice trails off.

Jaws creeps right up to me, climbs onto my sneakers, and settles in like it's naptime.

"You see?" Kristi is triumphant. "He knows who's the nicest."

"Will you cut it out?" Theo explodes at his sister. "You've been kissing up to Reef ever since he got here. It's embarrassing!"

"Both of you, cut it out," Mrs. Metzinger orders, "or I'll take you back to Memorial Hospital and trade you in for better kids!"

"Memorial Hospital?" I whip around to stare at Theo, dislodging the rabbit from my feet. "You were born at Memorial? Me too!"

"Memorial's the biggest hospital in the city," Mr. Metzinger points out. "Half the kids in the state were born there."

Theo and I exchange a long, meaningful look. We don't care about half the kids in the state. This means Theo and I were born on the very same day in the very same place. If we're searching for the cause of the Phenomenon, that's somewhere to start.

Jaws hops back onto my sneakers, shinnies up my leg, and settles himself on my knee.

CHAPTER EIGHTEEN

THEO METZINGER

Portia knows Declan all too well.

"I feel so bad for Reef, having to live with that creep," she confides to me at Neighborhood Harvest. "I mean, I feel sorry for Reef a hundred different ways, but this is one of them."

A local high school held a charity car wash over the weekend, with the proceeds going to the food bank. That money is currently in a lockbox behind Dmitri's desk. And it's no coincidence that Declan has been hanging around the office all afternoon. He even volunteered to mop the floor in there . . . which is suspicious, because Declan wouldn't know which end of a mop to hold. In more than a week on community service, Declan hasn't done a single thing other than goof off. His sudden interest in helping has everything to do with that lockbox.

Dmitri doesn't trust Declan either, but he's so busy that he doesn't have time to make the bank deposit. So Portia and I move our workstation close to the office door to keep an eye on things.

Declan perches on the corner of our table and leans into Portia's face. "I can take over for a little if you guys need a break."

"We don't," Portia replies firmly.

"They've got snacks in the locker room," Declan wheedles. "Cheez Doodles—good stuff."

"Those aren't snacks, they're groceries," I inform him. "They're part of the food we hand out."

"Am I talking to you, kid? I'm talking to Po-o-ortia." He stretches the name into a four-syllable word.

"We're not leaving you alone with that money, Declan," she tells him, plain talk.

Declan glares at her. "Typical. Perfect Portia—just like it's been since elementary school. The rest of us are garbage."

I move close to Declan and give him the stink eye. "Back off, man."

It's risky to stand up to him—especially since I have plenty of memories from Reef that tell me exactly what this jerk is capable of. I'm not the same wimpy Theo that I used to be. I've been in karate for months, and I must have biked about a billion miles by now, back and forth to Breezeway. Even Dad has remarked that I'm in great shape—and he's not the kind of guy to say that just to make me feel good.

Declan hops off the table and gets right in my face. He's skinny but definitely taller than me, with bony fists that look like they'd hurt. It's an important reminder: I can *act* tough; Declan really *is*.

"You've got a big mouth," he tells me, and walks away.

"And you've got a big problem, which is that we've got our eyes on you!" Portia calls after him.

Maybe we've convinced him not to mess with us. Or maybe he just backed down because beating me up wouldn't have looked good on his community service report.

The ride home from Breezeway hasn't gotten longer, but it has gotten darker. As we press deeper into the fall, I find myself pedaling home, squinting into the glow of my bike light. The gloom is less of a problem than the high beams of the cars coming toward me. I don't know what I'm going to do in December, when it's pitch-black by four thirty.

I round a traffic circle, preparing to lean into the next turn—and suddenly, I'm blank. There are three choices—three busy streets—and all three look equally wrong and equally right. I have no idea which one will lead me home.

I loop around the circle again. What's going on? I've made this trip so many times; I should be able to do it with my eyes closed. How can I have forgotten the route?

That last question fills me with understanding mixed with a hint of hysteria. I *haven't* forgotten the way. What happened is that my memory of it has landed in someone else's head.

By the time I complete my third circle, I'm totally lost. I can't even tell the way forward from the direction that would lead me back to Breezeway.

I pull over to the side and jump the curb to the safety of the sidewalk. Okay, this is bad, but it's not the end of the world. I've got a phone. All I have to do is put my address into the navigation app and the GPS will lead me home.

That's when I hit my next brick wall. *I can't remember my address!* I know my *house*—I picture the front porch, the flower garden I planted personally. I even see the number sixteen right next to the white-painted door. But sixteen *what*?

Part of me always knew this would happen eventually. The Phenomenon has been getting worse. Last Friday, Reef took a social studies test, and by the time he got to question one, he'd forgotten everything he'd studied for. He *did* study—I can confirm that for sure, because when he messaged me in a panic, I knew everything there was to know about Zambia. I tried to help him via text, but he still failed.

The thought of Reef offers me a lifeline. Just like I knew all those important facts about Zambia, he must know where I live. I call him and listen through an agonizing series of rings before the call goes to voice mail. I try again, mumbling "Pick up! Pick *up*!" as the rings begin again.

I almost pass out with relief when his voice comes on. "Sorry—I couldn't hear over the vacuum. What's up?"

I'm almost in tears. "Quick—where do I live?"

He sounds confused. "At your house."

"I mean my address," I insist. "What's my address?"

"Oh." He clues in. "Okay, don't freak out—"

I cut him off. "I'm lost, it's pitch-dark, and cars are whizzing by!"

"You live at Sixteen Forest Avenue," he supplies, speaking slowly and clearly. "Need me to repeat that?"

I key it into my GPS and a route appears on the screen. "Got it. Thanks a million."

The phone leads me for another mile or so, until, all at once, I know where I am. It's as if my mind is missing a whole chunk of information, but once I'm past the missing part, I'm fine. I'm like a computer with a batch of files deleted—only the files haven't disappeared. They've been sent to another computer named Reef, just as some of Reef's files have been sent to this computer: me.

As the Phenomenon progresses, so many files are going back and forth between us that it's interfering with the ability of our brains to operate.

The first thing they teach you in technology class is what happens when computers get too much corrupted data.

They crash.

CHAPTER NINETEEN

REEF MOODY

Willis is in charge of laundry at the Helmer house. I never get to sleep in on Saturdays because he shows up at the crack of dawn to ransack the hamper. There's always an argument because he has to pick up Declan's dirty socks and underwear off the floor.

"Come on, Dec! It's not far to the hamper! I'm not asking you to be Steph Curry!"

Declan goes straight back to sleep—if he bothered to wake up in the first place. But I usually drag myself down to the kitchen to get an early start on the day.

I'm slumped in my cornflakes, wondering if I'm going to need toothpicks to keep my eyes open, when Willis comes up from the laundry room and sits down next to me, his face grave.

"Is there something you want to say to me, Reef?"

I'm instantly alert. "What do you mean?"

He takes something out of his pocket and unfolds it on the table between us. I recognize it right away. It's a computer printout of the family photograph that sits on the coffee table in the living room. I made it myself three days ago. I must have forgotten it was in my pocket when I tossed my jeans into the hamper.

That was a serious mistake.

I know exactly why I printed that picture, but it isn't an explanation I can give Willis. First off, I labeled all five Helmers with their names. Why would I have to do that with people I live with and see every day? The way the Phenomenon has been going for Theo and me, you never know what you might forget next. Theo forgot his own address. I've been forgetting a lot at school—classes, teachers, even kids. Faces I've been seeing since kindergarten look blank to me. I got the office to print me a new copy of my schedule. I felt stupid asking for it in the middle of a semester, but I *need* that information. It has room numbers, subjects, and teachers' names. That's when I realized I need *notes* to get through my life.

Most important are the Helmers. So I made myself a study guide featuring Willis, Jenna, and their three kids. Under *Jenna*, it says *Mom's best friend*. Under Willis, I put *Thinks he's in charge*. From Liam and Carolyn, I drew arrows to a single comment: *Meh*. Declan has the most notations: *Goes to your school*, *Jerk*, and *Don't trust him*. I've also included everybody's phone numbers and the address of the house.

If I tell Willis I created this because I need a cheat sheet on the family, he's going to think I'm losing my mind. Which wouldn't be far from the truth—I'm losing large pieces of it to a kid named Theo who lives on the other side of town. Or he'll think I'm sassing him, which is even worse. I don't love everything about my life with the Helmers, but I'm smart enough to recognize that they didn't need to take me in. The loyalty from Jenna is incredible—considering that her loyalty is to Mom, not me.

"Did Jenna see this?" I ask in a small voice.

Willis shakes his head. "I didn't show it to her. I think she'd be hurt to find out how you feel about us."

It dawns on me: Since Willis can't see my cheat sheet for what it is, he thinks I created it as a putdown to his family! I have to find a way to tell him that's not true.

"It's nothing," I plead. "Just a bunch of scribbles I made on a bad day. Being able to live here with you guys—it's the only thing I've got right now. You and Jenna saved my life after Mom died—"

Willis looks surprised. "We're not asking for your appreciation. We just want you to be happy."

"I'm trying," I tell him honestly. "But a lot of things keep getting in the way."

He assumes I'm talking about his younger son. "I know it's tough with you and Dec. But it'll get better. I'm sure of it." A buzzer from the laundry room indicates that the dryer is finished. Willis ruffles my bedhead. "Good talk. We should probably get rid of this, though." He tears up my cheat sheet and drops it in the wastebasket before heading back down to the basement.

No sweat. I've already got a picture of it stored on my phone. Safer that way.

But there's one piece of info that's too vital to trust to a cheat sheet or even a phone. I pluck a fine Sharpie from the cup on the table, roll up my sleeve, and write Theo's phone number directly on my skin.

That's the only good thing about the Phenomenon. Nothing is ever entirely forgotten. It's all in *somebody's* memory—just not necessarily the person who needs to remember it. Whatever I'm missing, Theo has. Fact is, as long as I don't forget Theo, I'll always have backup.

Speaking of Theo, we have plans today. We're meeting at Memorial Hospital—the place we were born on March 23, twelve-plus years ago. I have no clue what we expect to find there. But if we're going to stop the Phenomenon, first we have to understand what's causing it. Theo and I grew up on opposite sides of town, went to different schools, and, as far as we can tell, never met. If anything happened to both of us at the same time, it had to have been when we were newborn babies together at Memorial.

The bus lets me off down the block from the hospital's main entrance, and by the time I make it to the door, Theo rolls up on his bike, navigating by his phone in the basket.

It's always kind of awkward when we see each other. We're not friends, but we're connected by something much closer. How do you face a guy who might remember the last time you squeezed a pimple, or spread itch cream in an embarrassing spot? I've experienced the stomachache he gets from eating raisin bran. And I'm in a perfect position to call baloney when he says he just wants to be friends with Portia. I have clear impressions of exactly how he feels about her.

"I called ahead," he says, locking up his bike. "Maternity is on the sixth floor."

I'm nervous. "What floor is psychiatry on? Because that's where they'll send us when we try to explain what we're here for."

He nods his understanding. "Obviously, we can't tell them everything. We'll have to wing it and see how it goes."

We enter, plucking masks from the dispenser by the doors. Just putting one on triggers a lot of awful connections in my mind—inhaling my own hot breath and hearing it too, directed toward my ears by the surgical fabric. Figures—I can't conjure an image of Mom without looking at my phone, but the antiseptic smell of the hospital's lobby sets off an avalanche of panic and loss. There's a cafeteria/gift shop on the main floor. I'm haunted by a memory of Jenna at the cash register, buying me a new phone case—not because I needed one, but because she felt so bad for me. She was crying and so was I. I look at Theo and I want to punch him, because he has so many of my experiences; why couldn't he have taken this horrible one too so I wouldn't have to relive it?

He senses that something is bothering me. "You can wait outside if you want. I can probably handle this by myself."

I grit my teeth. "I'll make it. Two heads are better than one." Especially two heads that are incomplete unless they're together.

Theo steps to the reception desk. "We need to go to Maternity," he tells the greeter.

She looks him up and down. "New big brother?"

"Yep," he replies without batting an eyelash.

"And a brother from another mother," I add with a confident smile that, come to think of it, no one can see behind my mask.

"You're fine to go to the nursery," she tells me. "But stay behind the glass. It's only immediate family in the patient rooms."

We take the elevator up to six, and when the doors open, an amazing sight greets us. The nursery is straight ahead, glassed in and safety sealed. I've obviously seen babies before, but never forty of them all in one place. And never so *little*!

"Are they all . . . twins?" Theo asks in an amazed voice.

It's a ridiculous question, but I understand exactly what he means. You can't tell one from the other. They're trussed up in blankets till they're the size of a football, so all you can see are scrunched red faces. It's impossible to tell the boys from the girls except by the blue or pink stickers on the Plexiglas bassinets. The only thing you know for sure is who's awake and who's not. The awake ones are screaming the nursery down.

It's a chaotic place, but also kind of cool. Every single one of those babies is a brand-new person, just starting out. And while most of them don't seem too happy about it, you still find yourself rooting for them.

I have to remind myself that we're here for a reason. "How's looking at babies supposed to teach us about the Phenomenon?" I mumble to Theo.

He shakes himself as if coming out of a trance. "Let's talk to one of the nurses."

There's a nurses' station at the beginning of a long hall that leads to patient rooms. I follow Theo to the bustling main desk. We have to wait to be noticed by a young man working at a computer keyboard.

"What can I do for you kids?"

Theo clears his throat. "We need some information."

The man's brow furrows. "Are you family? Big brothers?"

"We're babies," I blurt. "I mean, not anymore. We used to be babies."

"Welcome to the club. Me too."

Theo takes over. "You see, we were both born here. On the same day, March twenty-third, twelve years ago."

The nurse folds his arms across his chest. "What exactly are you trying to tell me?"

That's when I realize just how difficult this is going to be. How can you expect answers when you don't even know what the questions should be?

I take a stab at it. "We need to find of out if anything unusual happened that day."

Theo indicates the computer. "Maybe you could check your records?"

The man looks suspicious. "Sometimes lawyers come in here and make bogus claims—like the right kid didn't go home with the right mother. That's not you two, right?"

"No," Theo says quickly. "That's not it at all."

"To be honest," I add, "we're not really sure what we're looking for—just that we're looking for something. Do you remember anything weird from twelve and a half years ago?"

"Sure. I fell off my bike and scraped my knee," he replies instantly. "I was thirteen."

"Oh." Theo looks crestfallen. "Well, is there anyone older we can talk to? You know, who might have been working here back when we were born?"

A middle-aged nurse leans into the conversation. "There's been a lot of turnover in the maternity ward in the last ten or twelve years. The hospital had personnel problems, and most of the staff moved when they opened up City General. But back then, the head nurse was Nancy Turnbull."

"Can we talk to her?" Theo asks eagerly.

The older nurse shakes her head. "She left health care a couple of years ago. But I'm pretty sure she still lives in town. I saw her in the supermarket a few months back."

I whip out my phone. "Nancy Turnbull." A quick search of the city phone directory reveals eleven Turnbulls, none of them Nancy. "Are you sure? She isn't in the phone book."

She shrugs. "I think I heard she got married. Maybe she changed her name. Sorry."

The first guy stands up at his computer station. "You know, kids, we're pretty busy here. So if you're done, how about you let us get back to work?"

We take the hint and retreat to the elevator. The crying

coming from the nursery feels different now—like the babies are inviting us to join in.

I look at Theo, and for once, I don't need the Phenomenon to know exactly what he's thinking. This isn't a huge city like New York or LA, but there must be hundreds of Nancys in town. How are we ever going to find the right one?

CHAPTER TWENTY

THEO METZINGER

Dmitri has given up on the idea of Declan becoming useful in any way at Neighborhood Harvest: The plan now is to let the kid do whatever he wants so long as he doesn't get in the way. Eventually, he'll finish his time and be gone, hopefully leaving the food bank still standing.

The thing is, Declan has figured this out. He's awful, but you can't say he isn't smart. He's twice as obnoxious as before, since he knows Dmitri will keep signing his community service form anyway. He shows up in flip-flops and sunglasses. He clears off shelves to make room for his daily nap, folding up a delivery truck's tarpaulin to use as a mattress. There's barely a square inch of the building he hasn't slept in yet.

It makes Portia do a slow burn. "This can't be what the police had in mind when they sent him here," she complains to Dmitri.

"Let it go," Dmitri advises, stepping over one of Declan's sprawled legs. "The kid was born to do exactly what he's doing."

"What—nothing?" she demands. "Then he's falling short, since he's doing *less* than nothing! It's like we've got a cat. He's zero help; he prowls around like he owns the place—when he's awake. We do important work. Families depend on the food we provide. And he's making a big joke out of it."

A couple of times that week, a new kid shows up at Neighborhood Harvest—older and kind of tough looking. He says he just wants to use the bathroom, which is weird to begin with. Who does that at a food bank when there's a Starbucks with a public restroom three doors away?

He walks right by Declan, and not a word passes between them. But I get the feeling that they know each other. And if I don't trust Declan, I trust this new guy even less. First of all, he seems to make Declan a little nervous, which is something I've never seen before. And second, I have a vague sense that I remember this newcomer, but I can't quite place him. Which leads me to believe that it's Reef who remembers him. I can't pull up any details, or even the guy's name. But I detect an uneasy feeling toward this guy, which only adds to my suspicion about him.

The next time he comes in, I make sure to point him out to Portia.

"That's Konrad Sikorsky," she tells me in a low voice. "He's one of the only kids ever to get expelled from Delgado."

"We'd better tell Dmitri about him," I decide.

She bristles. "This is a food bank. We don't judge people here. Just because Konrad got into trouble at school doesn't mean he's looking for trouble here."

"Yeah, but it's kind of shady, don't you think?" I counter. "He comes in here to use the bathroom, noses around, and leaves. We're not a public rest stop."

"We're whatever people need us to be," she reminds me. "For all we know, he needs help and he's working up the courage to ask for it."

Just then, Konrad emerges from the bathroom, scanning his surroundings like a Secret Service agent escorting the president.

Portia intercepts him on the way to the exit. "Hi! Is there something I can help you with?"

Without even stopping, Konrad mumbles, "I'm good," sidesteps Portia, and is out the door and gone.

Over the next week, Konrad and Declan still don't exchange a single word during Konrad's continuing bathroom visits. But something strange begins to happen: The minute Konrad sets foot in our building, Declan—the laziest person in Neighborhood Harvest history—actually starts to *work*.

He packs boxes. He stocks shelves. He loads trucks. He becomes a model volunteer . . . until Konrad leaves again. Then, magically, he's back to his old useless self, loafing and napping.

"Wow," Portia remarks as Declan stacks metal shelves with soup cans in a clatter of machinelike efficiency. "He's finally getting into the spirit of this place. I never thought I'd see the day."

"You still haven't," I tell her sourly. "Just wait till Mr. Weak-Bladder takes off."

Sure enough, the minute Konrad is gone, Declan's "spirit" winks out like an ember in a downpour. He doesn't even stack the last can. He just drops it three inches short of the shelf and goes off to find his latest nesting area.

"What are you looking at?" he spits at Portia and me as he passes by en route to his tarp.

Portia never gives up. "You did a great job stacking those cans," she offers.

He tosses a long rolling burp over his shoulder.

One night, as soon as I get home from Breezeway, I call Reef and update him.

"He does work?" he repeats in a dubious tone. "Doesn't sound like the Declan I know."

"Only while this other kid's around," I report. "Konrad Sikorsky. They pretend they don't know each other, but I think they do."

"They know each other," Reef confirms grimly. "I saw them together. I'll bet Declan's scared to death of him."

I'm skeptical. "And he's showing his fear by doing his job?"

"Don't you see? He's doing his job because it's his way of escaping Konrad. Konrad is working some scam at the food bank, and he's recruited Declan to be his inside man. Now Declan wants to chicken out, but he doesn't have the guts to admit it."

"It still makes no sense," I argue. "What are they going to steal? Canned beans? A food bank has nothing but food. Oh, sure, there's money here and there to pay people and buy supplies, but it's not exactly big bucks. And anyway, Dmitri keeps it in a lockbox in the office."

Reef laughs without humor. "A lockbox is nothing to a guy like Sikorsky. He could be in and out of it in thirty seconds."

The next time I'm at Neighborhood Harvest, I slip into Dmitri's office and examine the lockbox. It's a big steel unit, thick-walled like a safe, bolted to the floor so no one can take off with it. At the top, the hasp is secured by a heavy padlock. Dmitri keeps the key with him.

I could never find a way to get into that box, but then again, I would never want to. Can I say the same about Konrad? Or Declan?

How bad is Declan really? Reef thinks he's the worst, and I can't blame him. But I get the feeling this Konrad character is a whole lot worse.

"Oh, hi, Theo. What can I do for you?" Dmitri steps into the office

Startled, I blurt the first thing that comes to my mind. "How safe is this thing?"

Dmitri is amused. "Why? Are you planning a heist?"

"No, it's just—" Yikes, here I am, about to accuse Konrad and Declan, when I'm the one who just got caught standing over the lockbox, asking how easy breaking into it would be.

Dmitri laughs. "I'm just pulling your chain, Theo. I know you're a good kid. Besides, if you robbed that thing right now, you know what you'd get? A grand total of eleven bucks and some loose change."

I'm relieved. Even if Konrad and Declan do break into the box, they won't get much out of it. "I guess nobody goes into the food bank business for the money."

"I wouldn't say that. Next week there's going to be two thousand bucks in there. The truck needs a new transmission. Sal at the garage will install it for free, but we have to pay cash for the parts."

I don't know how I stay upright as the realization settles in. Two thousand bucks—I don't know how Konrad got wind of it, but that must be the target.

And Declan . . . how does he fit into all this?

CHAPTER TWENTY-ONE

REEF MOODY

The most important person in the world is now Garth Avalon.

Who is he? Carolyn's boyfriend—her first. He's coming over tonight to watch a movie.

"And if you guys do anything to mess it up, you're dead!" Carolyn warns Liam, Declan, and me.

Jenna puts the threat a little more politely. "The four of you are getting older. Dating will be a part of your lives soon enough. All we're asking is that you give Carolyn and Garth the respect that you'd want for yourselves."

"Or you're dead!" Carolyn adds.

"Garth!" Declan sneers. "What kind of name is Garth?"

"A better one than Declan!" his sister snaps at him.

Liam has a complaint. "So our whole lives have to go on hold just because this dude is coming over?"

Willis is patient. "Nothing is on hold. You can live your lives. Just leave Carolyn and her friend alone. Is that too much to ask?"

Since I'm not a real Helmer, I don't have a lot of interest in the conversation. Personally, I don't care if Garth has a shrimp's head instead of a regular one. But later, when I go downstairs to vacuum, I catch Declan taking the Hoover out of the closet.

"Hey, that's my job. You're on garbage, remember?"

"You do garbage tonight," he tells me. "I'm in a vacuuming mood." He takes the machine and marches toward the door that leads to the living room.

I clue in. "You don't care about vacuuming! You just want to go in there and bust up Carolyn's date!"

"What's it to you, Reek?" he shoots back. "You're not even in this family!"

I wrap my arms around the Hoover and hold on. "Give. Me. That. Vacuum!"

Declan's bigger and stronger than me, but I hang there, determined to keep him from getting us both in trouble. I have no great love for Carolyn, but life in this house is usually easier when she gets her way.

"Let *go*!" Declan gives the Hoover an enormous yank, lifting me clean off the kitchen floor. The three of us—me, him, and the vacuum—tumble through the swinging door into the living room. My sneaker catches the cord and pulls the TV plug out of the wall, ending the movie. As we hit the carpet, the bag comes off the Hoover, sending up a dust cloud that fills the air like a thick fog.

On the couch, Garth dissolves into spasms of sneezing.

Carolyn leaps to her feet. *"Mo-o-o-om!"*

"It wasn't my fault," Declan mutters. "Reek tackled me."

The two of us are on the couch, getting yelled at by Jenna,

who could tear the aluminum siding off a house once she gets up to speed. Garth is gone. Turns out he has asthma and had to evacuate because of the dust.

"At least I apologized," I defend myself. "You just stood there and laughed."

"It's no big deal." Declan shrugs. "A first date—so what? It's not like she was going to marry this guy."

"How do you know?" Carolyn roars. "Maybe Garth was the one! Okay, he probably isn't, but it can never happen now because of two idiots! Maybe I was meant to be Mrs. Carolyn Avalon, née Helmer!"

That makes Declan laugh even harder. *"Nay!"* he brays. "You sound like a horse."

"*Née* means the last name you were born with, if you take your husband's name," Jenna explains sternly. "You see it in the wedding announcements in the newspaper. I'm Mrs. Jenna Helmer, née Blankenship."

"Really?" I snap to attention. "When you get married the newspaper prints your old name along with the new one?"

Carolyn throws up her hands. "My life is ruined and *this* is the conversation we're having?"

"Everybody calm down," Jenna orders.

But I can't calm down. I've just learned something monumental.

I know how we're going to find the nurse who was working at Memorial Hospital the day Theo and I were born.

The *Gazette*, our daily newspaper, has been publishing since 1893, but we don't have to go back as far as that. According to the people at Memorial Hospital, Nancy Turnbull wasn't married yet when she worked in the nursery. So Theo and I can start on the day we were born and work our way forward, sifting through all the wedding announcements in the *Gazette*'s online archives. The goal: Mrs. Nancy Somebody, née Turnbull. That's our missing nurse.

One problem, and it's a biggie: The archives aren't electronic—they're pictures of the actual newspaper pages themselves. So you can't search them by keyword. You have to go through them announcement by announcement. And that takes hours.

"I finished our birth year," Theo reports over the phone. "No Nancy Turnbull."

I draw a line through it, from January to December, on our chart. "Who knew so many people could get married in one little year?"

"Tell me about it," Theo groans. "My eyes are bugging out and my clicking finger has gone numb."

"Save your strength," I advise. "You have to harvest the last of the potatoes today."

His reply is wary. "I don't remember anything about that."

"Yes, you do."

"Oh—okay. Well, you finished the next year, right?"

"Not yet," I admit. "It must have been a really romantic time. Lots of weddings. But if you start on two years after, I'll take the year after that." Ugh.

We end the call and I return to the archive.

Mrs. Molly Bratsky, née Chanterelle . . . Mrs. Patricia Hall, no name change . . . Mrs. Kathleen Sigurdssen, née Fortunoff . . .

It's so boring that my mind shuts down, and I have to hope I'm not skimming over the very thing I'm looking for. I'd hate to have to start this over again. And on top of it all, I can't shake the feeling that I should be picking potatoes, even though I know that's Theo and not me.

I try to keep my focus on the screen and not the voices outside my window—until I hear one word that grabs my full attention: *"Konrad."*

I rush over and peer through the blinds. Declan is directly below, speaking urgently into his phone. Soundlessly, I ease open the sash and eavesdrop.

"Listen, man!" Declan's voice is pleading. "It's too risky! I'm not at that place for fun, you know. The court sent me there!"

This is it: proof that Declan and Konrad are in cahoots!

The conversation goes on, although I can only hear Declan's side. "I'm *not* being a wuss! Can't you see how this is going to go? You'll walk away with the money, and I'll be stuck trying to explain what happened to the cops! . . . I know you're good for my cut. That's not what this is about . . . I'm *not* accusing you of stiffing me! Konrad, listen—"

Gazing down on the exchange, I almost feel bad for Declan. Oh, sure, he deserves whatever he gets. This is his dishonesty and sleaze catching up with him.

But he sounds pretty scared now—and he should be.

However bad Declan is, triple it and you've got Konrad. Whatever they're planning, Declan wants to call it off. And okay, it's not because he suddenly learned the difference between right and wrong. Fact is, he's trying to do the right thing, even if it's for the wrong reasons—like not getting himself thrown in juvie.

Declan is sputtering now, apologizing for trying to back out, swearing loyalty to the plan, all but blubbering.

I close the window. Not my problem. What do I care about Declan? Every time I hand over another twenty to Latimore, I'm reminded of what the guy did to me.

But I do care about Jenna, and even Willis. And while Declan seems like a monster to me, I'll bet Konrad seems like a monster to *him*.

Having a monster pushing you around is something I can definitely sympathize with.

I go downstairs and let myself outside.

Declan is slumped on the steps, still staring at his phone, looking stunned. When he sees me, he spits out, "Beat it, Reek!"

I'm not sure why I sit down next to him. I've never supported him before and he's never wanted my support. But something feels different.

Suddenly, he looks alarmed. "What did you hear?"

I'm tempted to lie. If he knows I've been eavesdropping, Declan is likely to get back at me times ten if it's the last thing he does. But somehow, I find the guts to say, "That was Konrad, right? Konrad Sikorsky?"

His eyes widen, first in shock, then in rage. Half of me

wants to start running. This is the guy who threw a rock at my head when I was minding my own business. Minding *his* business has to be a more serious offense.

The anger builds in him until I'm positive I'm about to get punched. Then, all at once, he deflates like a squashed football. "What would you know about a guy like Konrad? Goody-goody Reek, my mother's pet, who always does what he's told and never breaks a rule."

I'm taken aback. Is that how he sees me? Jenna's *pet*?

I can't resist throwing it in his face. "I'm pretty sure swiping the principal's pocketbook isn't something a goody-goody does."

He studies his sneakers. "You don't do that kind of stuff! That's why my mother loves you more than her own son! You're *good*! You're not"—his voice is suddenly quiet—"like me."

It strikes me for the first time: When I accused Declan of swiping Latimore's purse, he never challenged how I knew that. Of course I saw him as a thief because everyone sees him as a thief. That's how he sees himself.

"You're not like Konrad," I offer. "At least you don't have to be."

"It's too late," he mourns. "Konrad's not the kind of guy you say no to. Not now. I can't back out."

"Yeah, you can. Nothing's done till it's done. And you haven't done anything yet."

His eyes narrow. "How much do you know?"

I hesitate. If I reveal that my source of information at the food bank is Theo, then I'll have to explain the connection between the two of us. And I really don't want to do that. I'm not sure I even can—not in a way that anybody would ever believe.

So I reply, "Just that you can't throw your life away because of Konrad Sikorsky."

"It's not that simple," he shoots back. "Konrad's dangerous. Who knows what he might do to me? I can't say yes, but I can't say no either. Those are the only two choices."

"You could go to the police," I suggest.

"Oh, that's great!" he explodes. "They love me so much already! And what we're going to do—the people we're doing it to—they don't forgive you for stuff like that. I shouldn't forgive myself. It's my own fault—what was I thinking?"

I make one final effort. "This is too big for you to face alone. Maybe you should talk to Willis and Jenna."

It's the one sentence that could bring him back to life. He leaps to his feet and glares down at me. "That's the stupidest thing I've ever heard! As dumb as I was to get myself into this, at least I'm not as dumb as you!" He storms into the house, slamming the door so hard that I bounce on the stoop.

I stand up slowly, reflecting on the longest conversation I've ever had with Declan, even though we've been sharing a room for a year. He's probably right that I'm not too bright. Because in spite of everything, I'm determined to help him get through this.

Now, why would I want to do that after the way he's treated me? The way he *still* treats me! Maybe the answer came from Declan's own mouth: "You're *good*." It surprised me—not just because it was a compliment, but because I never think of myself that way.

If I'm good, it's thanks to my mother—the things she taught me, the values she lived by. *That's* a part of Mom that no phenomenon can ever steal from me. My memory of her may be disappearing, but in this one way, she'll always still be here. Helping the jerk who makes my life miserable is part of that.

There's only one problem: How?

CHAPTER TWENTY-TWO

THEO METZINGER

The 1:42 bus is already loading when I ride up to the depot. I see Reef at the back of the line, impatiently checking the time on his phone.

I snap the lock around a bar on the bike rack and run to join him.

"You're late," he accuses as we board and swipe our cards.

We take seats in the front row behind the driver. "Sorry," I tell him. "I got stuck on the phone. Portia's ticked off at me. I guess we had plans this morning and I totally blanked on it."

"Well, maybe not *totally*," Reef replies meaningfully.

"You *knew*?" I feel a stab of anger.

"You were meeting for fro-yo at eleven," he explains with just a hint of a smirk.

"Aw, come on! If you remember it, that means I forgot! We're supposed to remind each other about things like that!"

Reef folds his arms in front of him. "Maybe I'd be more honest with you if you'd be more honest with me. Like about what's going on between you and Portia."

"Nothing's going on between Portia and me," I insist. "We're just friends who volunteer together. And anyway, what's it to you? You don't even like her."

He gives me a stonewalling stare and then turns his attention out the bus window at the stores and restaurants scrolling by. I want to say more—like how, in our situation, if we don't share information about each other's memories, we're both in big trouble. It goes far beyond a missed fro-yo date. I forgot Dr. Abagnale's name last week and spent twenty minutes in the lobby of her building, trying to figure out which office was hers. If this keeps up, we're going to need each other just to get through our day-to-day lives. Surely Reef is experiencing that too.

Lately, I've been having more and more memories of the woman I know is his mother. That must mean he's losing them. I know I should share them with him, but he's so touchy on the subject that we always end up fighting. We can't fight today. This trip is too important.

We finally found Nancy Turnbull in the newspaper wedding announcements. She got married five years ago and changed her name to Nancy Giamatti. We looked up her address, and she lives in a suburb called Whitfield, about seven miles outside of town. That's our destination. If anybody can tell us what was going on at Memorial Hospital the day we were born, it's her.

"Hope she's home," Reef comments nervously as our bus exits the city limits and tools along the wide boulevards and tree-shaded neighborhoods of Whitfield. "We should have called ahead."

"I would have," I tell him, "if I could have figured out a way to tell her what we want to know. At least when we're standing on her doorstep, she'll be able to see that we're not a couple of scammers or something."

"If she's there at all. We're going to look pretty ridiculous if she's away in Australia for the next three months."

We're both tracking the bus's progress on our phones, and when we get close to the Giamattis' address, I pull the cord to request a stop. The driver lets us out and we continue on foot, still navigating by GPS. Finally, we're standing in front of a low, rambling ranch house about a quarter mile in from the main road.

"Car in the driveway," Reef notes optimistically. "Good sign."

As I ring the doorbell, my guts are churning like a storm at sea. We've done it—we've found the neonatal nurse who was on duty when Reef and I were born. But is she going to be able to help us? Who knows if she'll remember what was going on in a busy maternity ward over twelve years ago? And even if she does, will it do us any good? The Phenomenon is so unnatural, so bizarre, so *impossible*—how can we ask anyone to reach back in their memory and identify a cause for it? What explanation could there possibly be for something that shouldn't be happening in the first place?

First we hear a dog barking, followed by a woman's voice: "Quiet, Hector!" A moment later, the door opens and there she is: Nancy Turnbull Giamatti. I expected her to be kind of grandmotherly, since she was a working nurse back when Reef and I were born. Still, that was only twelve years ago, which isn't super long in adult time. This lady is probably fiftyish, older than my parents, but not by much. She's hanging on with both hands to the collar of a golden retriever.

We stand there, staring at her like dopes.

Enough silence goes by that she laughs. "Well, you rang the bell, so I assume you want something."

Reef finally finds his voice. "Nancy Turnbull?"

"I used to be," she replies. "Who wants to know?"

"The nurse?" I persist.

"That's me. What's all this about?"

"We're your babies. I mean, we used to be babies. And you were our nurse. You know—back when we first got born."

She frowns. "Now, how would you know that—and don't say it's because you remember my movie-star good looks and nimble-fingered diapering."

I stammer out a short version of our visit to Memorial Hospital and our journey through the wedding announcements in the *Gazette*.

She takes all this in, giving us a thorough once-over with her eyes to determine whether we're dangerous stalkers. At last, she says, "I guess you really *are* my babies. What dates were you born?"

"Just one date," Reef supplies. "March twenty-third, twelve years ago."

She nods. "That makes sense. I worked in the nursery back then. So you tracked me down. Now what?"

I take a deep breath. Reef and I both agree that there's no sense trying to tell Nancy Giamatti about the Phenomenon.

That's a surefire way to get the door slammed in our faces. But we have to give her just enough that she'll want to help us.

"The two of us never met until a few weeks ago," I begin carefully. "We grew up on opposite sides of town and went to different schools. But we have a lot of things in common. Weird things—things there's no explanation for. We know stuff about each other, almost like there's a connection between us. And as far as we can tell, the only time we were ever together was as newborns at Memorial Hospital."

"You boys have certainly done your homework," she tells us. "But what is it you think I can do for you?"

Reef takes over. "We're trying to figure out what this connection is and how it got started. And we were wondering if maybe something unusual happened at the hospital when we were there."

She doesn't answer right away, so I put in, "I know that sounds a little science-fiction-y. But anything you remember about that day could be a clue for us."

"You boys are probably reading too much into this," she says at last. "A lot of what we see as hugely important turns out to be nothing more than coincidence."

Reef and I exchange an agonized glance. If this nice lady sends us away with a nurse-like pat on the head, we'll be right back where we started—nowhere. Nancy Giamatti is our only lead. Without her, we're sunk.

She goes on. "I'll tell you what. I used to keep a journal when I was a young nurse at Memorial. Come inside, have a cookie, and I'll see if it says anything about that day. But don't get your hopes up. Most shifts at maternity are pretty boring, if you don't count the crying."

She invites us into her shiny white kitchen, sits us down with a plate of homemade cookies, and heads upstairs to get her diary.

I reach for a cookie, which brings a low growl from Hector, who's seated at attention on the kitchen floor like a guard dog, ready to pounce. I withdraw my hand like it's been burned.

Reef helps himself to a cookie and munches it down. Hector makes no complaint. I think of Jaws, my rabbit nemesis who curls up on Reef with something approaching love. What is it about Reef and the four-legged? Does he have some special aura or something?

"Good cookies," Reef comments. "Chocolate chip, my favorite." He reaches down to scratch Hector behind one ear.

Nurse Giamatti comes into the kitchen, flipping through an overstuffed leather-bound diary. "March twenty-third," she says with a strange look on her face. "You boys may be onto something after all."

"What is it?" I ask anxiously.

"We had a lot of births that day," she explains. "I remember because we had to use incubators as extra cribs. We even doubled up in one of them—two little boys."

"Us?" Reef breathes.

"Could be. But that's not all. That night, we had a tremendous thunderstorm and the hospital was struck by lightning. When I came in for my shift the next day, the nursery was running on backup generator power. The electrical system was fried. It's a miracle no one was hurt."

"Except us," Reef says in an awed tone.

"Don't you read anything into that," she cautions. "No matter what happened, there were no ill effects suffered by any of our babies. Of course we checked everyone out—we're a hospital, after all. It's just what I said before: coincidence. Right?"

Reef and I lock eyes. Two babies, isolated together. A lightning strike. Electricity pulsing through the confined space of an incubator. A pathway opened between two unformed minds.

It's impossible. It defies medical science.

But what other answer could there be?

CHAPTER TWENTY-THREE

REEF MOODY

Why do I always get stuck with people I can't stand?

Like Declan, obviously. But at least all I have to share with him is a room. With Theo, it's getting to the point where we almost share the same brain. I'll have a memory—good, bad, whatever—and then it'll take me half the day to puzzle out whether it comes from my life or his. If the Phenomenon keeps getting worse, it's going to be impossible to keep track of where he stops and I start.

Not that Theo is as bad as Declan. But he's such a know-it-all and so pushy. Look at the way he took over the whole conversation with Nancy Giamatti. And for a know-it-all, he can't seem to understand that I just want to be left alone. I haven't got space in my life for an un-best friend who's roaming free inside my head. I'm already saddled with an un-family; I don't need an un-BFF. Fact is, the only person I'd do anything to be saddled with is out of reach, both in real life and in my memory.

But I'm stuck with Theo just as surely as I'm stuck with Declan and the other Helmers. More, even. If I blow off Theo, I won't be rid of him. His memories will still be swirling around my head and mine will be swirling around his. I've even picked up a couple of his memories that involve *me*. That's a trip—remembering meeting *yourself*, but from somebody else's point of view.

The only way to break free of Theo would be to undo what brought us together in the first place—the Phenomenon. And who knows if that's even possible?

"Well, at least we sort of understand how it might have happened," Theo muses. "We took a lightning strike together when we were babies."

After our meeting with Nurse Giamatti, we go back to the Helmer house, since I live close to the bus station where Theo left his bike. I'm perched on my bed, and Theo is at the desk. The two of us are on our phones, googling like crazy, desperate to follow up on what we just learned. All we can confirm so far is that Memorial Hospital really was struck by lightning when the two of us were a few hours old. And we both looked up what an incubator is—a sealed Plexiglas bassinet with temperature and oxygen controls.

"In other words, we know nothing," I tell him. "We can't even be sure that those two babies were us."

"It had to be," Theo decides in his know-it-all way. "Something must have happened to both of us at the same time to cause the Phenomenon. That hospital was the only time we were together before a few weeks ago. Throw two kids in an incubator and add a lightning strike—it's us, all right."

I nod reluctantly. "Nurse Giamatti talked about coincidences, but it doesn't seem like this could be one." I peer at my phone screen, which shows a diagram of how an incubator works. It's easy to picture the lightning creating a power surge that travels through the wires to the bassinet, where two helpless babies are surrounded by electricity. "But is that even a thing? Minds connected by lightning? How come it isn't on the internet or in the news?"

"Maybe it never happened before," Theo suggests. "Maybe we're the only ones."

In kindergarten, when they tell you that you're special and unique, I bet they don't mean this. Lucky us.

I have another question. "And why is it just starting now? If lightning linked our minds when we were babies, shouldn't the Phenomenon have been going on our whole lives?"

"It could be the kind of thing that gets triggered by puberty—or at least that's when the effect gets too big to ignore." He shrugs. "We might never know for sure. What we have to decide is this: So far, we've been keeping everything to ourselves. But maybe there are people who could help us. Doctors. Scientists. Brainiacs."

I shake my head vehemently. "I'm never letting a bunch of adults invade my life again. Been there, done that when Mom died."

He nods his understanding. "Best case, nobody would believe us. Worst, we'd both end up connected to electrodes or something."

Gloomy silence. We agree on what we can't do. That doesn't get us a millimeter closer to figuring out what we *can*.

The door is kicked open hard enough to slam the knob against the wall. Declan storms into the room, already scowling. "Don't talk to me, Reek! I don't want to hear—" He stops dead, staring at Theo. "What's *he* doing here?"

It hits me: Declan knows Theo from Neighborhood Harvest. He's never seen the two of us together before. "Theo and I are friends," I supply.

"You're so dumb! This kid isn't your friend—he's from the food bank! He's here to spy on me!"

"I'm not spying," Theo defends himself. "But maybe I should be."

Declan grabs Theo by the wrist and hauls him to his feet. "Get out of here, man! Get out of my house!"

I jump up and separate them. "It's my house too, you know!"

Declan's so agitated that he misses the opportunity to point out whose house this is and whose it isn't. "He's playing you, Reek! He's only hanging around you to get to me—to rat me out to the cops!"

"The cops?" I echo. "Is this about *Sikorsky*?"

Declan droops like a birthday candle that melts too fast. "It's no use. They *know*," he moans, glaring at Theo. "I can't go through with it and I can't get out of it!"

"You *can* get out of it," I tell him. "We'll help you."

"You?" He points at Theo. "*He's* one of *them*!"

"I'm not," Theo insists. "I volunteer at the food bank and I'm Reef's friend. That's it—honest."

Declan's eyes widen, and I wonder if he's going to try to weasel out of what he already said. Then his face crumples like a toddler about to bawl. "No one can help me. I can't even help myself."

"You could go to the police," I suggest. "Warn them about what's going to happen."

He shakes his head miserably. "They can't arrest Konrad for what he hasn't done yet. He'll come after me—and, believe me, he's worse than the cops."

Theo looks thoughtful. "So what we need is a way to protect Neighborhood Harvest and also to protect you from Konrad."

"Dream on." Declan sighs. "I'm supposed to hide when the food bank closes so I can let Konrad in after dark. When he shows up, I'd better be there, or I've got a target on my head."

Theo and I exchange a look. Declan can easily stop the robbery. All he has to do is not show up. But then he'd be making an enemy of the most dangerous kid in town.

"When's all this supposed to happen?" I ask.

Declan swallows hard. "Tomorrow night."

CHAPTER TWENTY-FOUR

THEO METZINGER

I'm always happy to see Portia, but this is different—like I'm surprised and thrilled that she noticed me. She seems different too. Long straight hair, bangs. Maybe a little shorter . . .

When the classroom eases into focus around her, it comes to me: I've never gone to school with Portia. This isn't my memory.

"I'm having some people over for my birthday next Saturday," she says with a dazzling smile. "I hope you can make it."

It may be from a long time ago, but it's classic Portia—friendly, open, and a hundred percent confident: *You're going to be ecstatic to get this invitation and of course you're going to say yes.*

"Thanks, Portia," I reply in Reef's voice. "I'll be there."

"Six o'clock," she adds. "Don't be late."

I can feel Reef's excitement. It's all he can do to keep himself from dancing as she walks away. He must have really liked her. What happened? I get slapped down if I even mention her.

"Theo." It's Portia's voice—not from the memory. Portia today.

I startle and bang my knee on the underside of the front desk at Neighborhood Harvest. "Ow!"

She laughs. "You're daydreaming again, Basket Case. Time to go. We're closing up."

All around the warehouse, volunteers are restocking unclaimed groceries and finishing last-minute tasks. I look around for Declan, but there's no sign of him. To be honest, I'm not sure if he's already hiding, or if he's lost his nerve.

Dmitri already has his jacket on. "Okay, everybody, let's move. I want to make it home on time for a change, since I'll be here early tomorrow. We're finally getting the truck fixed."

I think of all that money sitting in the lockbox and know that, somewhere, Konrad Sikorsky is thinking about it too.

When Dmitri closes the heavy door and clicks the dead bolt, the snap echoes up and down the street. Or maybe it just sounds that way to me because I know what's coming.

Portia suggests that we go for fro-yo, but I make up an excuse about rushing home to study. I'm glad to get her out of the way. She doesn't need to be involved in this.

I bike over to Reef's and we sweat out the next hour up in his room.

The waiting is nerve-wracking, so conversation between us is pretty limited. My eyes are drawn to a framed photograph on his nightstand. His mom, distorted by a spiderweb of cracked glass, damage courtesy of Declan.

"Why are you helping him?" I ask honestly. "I'm doing it for Neighborhood Harvest. What's your excuse?"

"You tell me," he shoots back irritably. "I forgot, so you must know."

"Because his family adopted you," I suggest.

"Nobody adopted me. I'm just allowed to live here, that's all."

"Fine. They took you in," I amend.

He's silent for a moment. Then he says, "You want to hear something messed up? The minute I heard Declan was in trouble, I knew I had to help him. I didn't think about all the lousy things he does to me. How's that for pathetic?"

I don't answer, but to me, it's not pathetic at all. It's the kind of thing that shows you're basically good, even though bad things have happened you. It might not make you popular or help you rule the school or anything like that. But maybe it explains why a rabbit or somebody's little sister is drawn to you. There are definitely worse people to be trapped in a phenomenon with.

Reef checks his phone. "Seven fifteen. We should go."

We make our way through the dark streets to Neighborhood Harvest and sneak around the back to the loading dock. The truck is parked there, waiting for its new engine . . . which is going to be paid for by money that may or may not still be in the lockbox tomorrow, depending on our actions tonight.

I tap lightly against the metal bay door, three raps followed by two—the secret knock. Declan already told us that he and Konrad don't have a secret knock. "That kind of thing is only for goofballs like you two," he assured us. Thanks, Dec. We love you too.

We wait in the gloom, still not certain that Declan is going to be there. Then we hear the rattle of the mechanism, and the door lifts about a foot and a half. We roll underneath into the light of Declan's phone. He brings the door back down again.

"What took you so long?" he hisses angrily. "I've been going out of my tree!"

It might be the harsh shadows, but he looks like an oversized raccoon—sunken eyes surrounded by dark circles. He probably hasn't been sleeping. When a juvenile delinquent wannabe gets mixed up with a real crook like Konrad, it shows him exactly how much of a crook he *isn't*. Except that by the time Declan learned that lesson, he was already in too deep and couldn't get himself out.

"You said Konrad's coming around eight," I tell him. "That's half an hour away."

Declan calms down a little after that. What he does next is totally unexpected: He wraps his arms around Reef and pulls him into an awkward hug.

Reef's eyes pop wide open and his ears glow like fireplace coals. I don't blame him for being surprised. When Declan came at him, he probably thought he was about to be tackled.

"It's okay, man," Reef manages finally. "We got this."

Eventually, they get disentangled and Reef and I take our positions in our hiding place—the office closet. We leave the door slightly open so we have a clear view of the lockbox bolted to the floor behind Dmitri's desk.

Declan won't leave us, probably because he's afraid to

be alone. He paces the floor, a nervous wreck, checking and rechecking the time on his phone. We have to kick him out because the glow from the screen is making it impossible for us to develop any kind of night sight.

"Where am I supposed to go?" he complains—like there isn't a six-thousand-square-foot warehouse all around us.

"Wait by the door," I advise, "so you don't miss Konrad when he comes."

He isn't gone more than a few minutes when we hear pounding on metal.

"He's early!" Reef whispers.

I sense the panic in his voice, and it matches my own. Crouching in a dark closet isn't fun, but suddenly, I'd give anything for it to last a little longer.

The rattling mechanism of the loading bay door opening and then closing is our signal: Konrad is in the building.

Footsteps approach, and so do two voices. Declan whispers urgently, but Konrad is speaking in his normal voice, bold as brass.

"Just stay out of my way, Helmer. It'll all be over soon, and you can go running home to Mommy."

Then Konrad is in the office. I squint at him through the gap in the closet door. He's wearing a trench coat that extends below his knees. From under it, he produces a long bolt cutter and positions the blades around the padlock that secures the lockbox on the floor.

It's a good thing Reef is here, because I'm frozen. For some reason, I assumed that getting at the money would be a long process that involved burglar tools or at least a hairpin. But now I realize that a split second from now, the bolt cutters will snap the lock and the cash will be gone.

Reef explodes out of the closet, phone in hand. When he takes the picture, the flash is like a supernova, lighting up the office and the warehouse beyond it.

Konrad couldn't be more shocked if we'd put ten thousand volts through him. He lifts a couple of feet off the ground, coming down in the direction of the phantom flash. "Who's there?"

It's my turn to take a picture. On my screen, I can see that I've captured him face on, the bolt cutters clearly visible.

"If that money disappears," Reef warns, "the cops are going to get a photo of you busting into the lockbox."

With a growl, Konrad leaps forward and takes a swing at us with the bolt cutters. We jump back out of reach, but I can feel the breeze as the heavy tool whizzes by where my head used to be.

Konrad grabs my wrist and squeezes so hard that I relax my grip and my phone clatters to the floor.

"Go ahead—erase it!" I shout. "I've already sent it to everybody on my contact list!"

"You're bluffing!" Konrad sneers.

"But I'm not!" Reef's fingers dance across his phone screen.

"You!" Furious recognition floods into Konrad's features. He wheels to face Declan in the doorway. "That's the stray your mama took in off the street!"

"Cut it out, Konrad." Declan's words sound uncertain and weak.

“You set me up!” Konrad accuses, advancing menacingly on Declan.

“If you touch him, I’ll send this picture to the cops!” Reef threatens.

Outnumbered and surrounded, Konrad spins on his heel and makes a run at Reef. Declan springs into action at last, grasping his former partner from behind and holding on. As they struggle, the bolt cutters drop to the tiles between their feet.

“Lay—off—my—brother!” Declan gasps, straining with effort.

I throw myself into the fray. With great difficulty, Declan and I wrestle Konrad away from Reef and hurl him toward the office door.

He staggers back a few steps and snarls, “This isn’t over!”

I pluck my phone off the floor and hold it up. “If anything happens to any of us, you’re going to spend the rest of your teenage years locked up!”

For an instant, it looks as if he’s going to make another run at us. Then he snatches up the fallen bolt cutters and storms off, exiting Neighborhood Harvest through the front door.

Declan is terrified. “He’s going to come after me!”

“No—we’re good!” Reef soothes him. “We’ve got the pictures.”

“You think a guy like Konrad is scared of *pictures*?” Declan demands. “We laid *hands* on him. You heard what he said: *This isn’t over!*”

We examine the photos on our phones. They're pretty incriminating, especially Reef's. He managed to capture Konrad crouched over the lockbox, the blades of the bolt cutter opened wide to snap off the lock. It couldn't be more perfect if we asked the guy to pose in the act of committing the crime.

"We'll send a copy of this to Konrad," I decide. "He'll leave us alone. He's vicious, but he's not stupid."

Declan calms down a little then.

"The money is safe," I announce. "Guaranteed. Even if Konrad can break in by himself, he'd never dare steal it. Not when we have these pictures."

I sound confident, but as I head to the bathroom, I can feel the contents of my stomach rising up into my throat. I pull the door shut behind me and dry-heave into the sink.

It's over. We did it. We're okay.

I splash cold water on my face and marvel at how normal I look in the mirror.

How do I seem so cool, so calm when I'm really scared out of my wits? What experience from my life could possibly have prepared me for a showdown with a hardened criminal like Konrad?

Instantly, the memory pops into my mind: I'm younger, uncomfortable in an ill-fitting suit, watching a flower-draped casket lowered into the ground. It's not my memory—it's Reef's. I've experienced it dozens of times in the course of the Phenomenon, maybe because it's his strongest memory—or at least the most awful.

Worst of all is the sadness that comes with it, pressing down like a thousand-pound weight, blotting out any light until all that's left is pure suffering.

Yeah, tonight is pretty so-what-else-is-new compared with that.

CHAPTER TWENTY-FIVE

REEF MOODY

It's been more than a week since the face-off at Neighborhood Harvest, and not a peep out of Konrad Sikorsky. Looks like our blackmail is working. Declan is still nervous. Me, not so much. Konrad would never risk our pictures falling into the hands of the police.

It's the same old Declan, yet in a way it isn't. Still surly, still complaining full-time, still communicating by means of a series of grunts. What's different is his use of the word *we*—meaning him and me, like we're a team and always have been. *We* need a ride to school from that lazy so-and-so Liam, who can't be bothered to hang around three extra minutes until we're ready; *we* need Willis to quit running the dryer on high, which is eating the logos off our T-shirts; *we* are sick of vacuuming and garbage duty and it's time for others to do their fair share around here.

"You can't just dump all the dirty jobs on Reef and me," he argues.

Notice that I'm not Reek anymore. I'm pretty sure my smell hasn't changed. The difference is Declan. Plus, Theo says he's doing a good job at the food bank—he's actually helping instead of lying around getting in the way. As expected,

Konrad has stopped showing up to use the bathroom. And since the truck has been fixed, all that money is gone from the lockbox anyway.

I keep thinking back to our struggle with Konrad and the bolt cutters. Declan, voice rasping: *"Lay—off—my—brother!"*

His *brother*? That's how he sees me?

Or was Declan so freaked out at that moment that he had no idea what he was saying?

When I get called to the office, my groan rattles the windows. At this point, my sense of Delgado is mixed up with memories of every school Theo went to. I doubt I could find Latimore with GPS. Every twist and turn in the halls seems right and wrong at the same time.

Know how I get there? By following the hurricane evacuation arrows. Sure enough, there's the office not too far in from the front door. Before I enter, I pen a little map of the way back to class on the palm of my hand. I'm getting pretty good at little reminders like that. They're not perfect, but they help me get through the day.

"What are you doing?"

Uh-oh. Latimore stands at the open door, watching me.

"Nothing." I jam the pen in my pocket and hold my hand behind my back.

"You kids and your homemade tattoos," she clucks disapprovingly. "Don't you know that can get infected if you break the skin?" She leads me into her office and perches on the edge of her desk. "Now, is there something you'd like to tell me?"

That's a loaded question for any principal to ask a kid. I'd like to tell her a lot of stuff. I'd like to tell her to take a flying leap at the moon. But that's the kind of thing that keeps a guy on vacuuming for life.

So I say, "I don't know what you mean."

She hands me an envelope. In it is a folded paper that declares in smudged block capitals:

REEF MOODY
DID NOT STEAL
YOUR POCKETBOOK!!!

Attached with a paper clip are three twenty-dollar bills—exactly the amount I still owe her.

Declan—it has to be. First of all, who besides Declan could get so many smudges and smears on a seven-word message? But it's exactly him. Even when he tries to do the right thing, he does it the wrong way. A normal person would confess and take the heat. Not Declan. I almost understand. He's finally straightening out his life; the last thing he needs is a big stink at school. So the best he can think of is to pay the rest of my tab and write an anonymous note declaring me innocent.

"Do you know who this might be from?" the principal asks.

I don't lie, but I don't answer either.

She lets the uncomfortable silence drag on. I can't meet her eyes, so I stare at my sneakers.

"Very well," she says finally. "I think I might understand what happened here."

I look up sharply. "But this is over, right? I'm not in trouble anymore and neither is . . . anybody else?"

She reaches out her hand and we shake solemnly.

"Do you remember anything special about the day I was born?"

A couple of days later, I'm at the Metzinger house when Theo asks his mom that question.

"Of course," Mrs. Metzinger replies with a big smile. "That was when I first became a mother. Nothing's more special than that."

"Yeah, but I mean something different," Theo persists. "You know, like really bad weather?"

Theo's dad shrugs. "Who cares about weather? Now when *Kristi* was born—that I remember perfectly. It was Super Bowl Sunday. Mom didn't go into labor until the final whistle, so I caught every play. And by morning, I had a bouncing baby daughter."

"Yeah, but what about *me*?" Theo persists.

"Football season was over by then," Mr. Metzinger replies. "It was March Madness."

"The hospital got struck by lightning," Theo tells them in exasperation. "It was the worst thunderstorm to hit the city in, like, forever."

"How would you know that?" his mother asks. "You were zero."

I pluck a tortilla chip from the bowl and reach for the salsa. The cuff of my sleeve rides up past my wrist, revealing row upon row of handwritten notes halfway up my arm.

Theo's parents regard me disapprovingly. After that, dinner is pretty awkward. They probably think I've covered myself with crib notes to help me cheat on a test. The worst part is I can't even defend myself. How can I ever explain what they're really for?

After dinner, we head upstairs, and Theo shows me his own notes. He keeps them on his phone—pages of messages, reminders, maps, and diagrams. "A lot of it's passwords," he admits. "I can't tell the difference between yours and mine anymore. I know it's the least of our problems, but I keep getting locked out of TikTok."

"I've started writing on my legs because my arms are full," I say seriously. "If this keeps up, I'll have to drop my pants to remember my locker combination. That'll be a hit with the kids at school."

Theo slumps on his bed. "It's getting bad."

"It's *already* bad."

"I mean bad like we have to do something about it. We can't keep this a secret forever. People are going to start to notice how confused we are."

I'm bitter. "What can we do? Build a time machine so we can go back to the hospital and pull one of our baby selves out of that incubator? Or a mad scientist gizmo to zap us back to normal?"

He sits back up, a thoughtful expression on his face. "It's not impossible, you know."

"You know the Basket Case thing is a joke, right?"

"I'm serious," he insists. "Electricity did this to us. Maybe electricity can undo it."

"You mean lick a battery? Or pee on an electric fence?"

He shakes his head. "I mean create the same conditions we were in the night we were born."

"Get a grip!" I explode. "We were in an incubator for newborn babies! We could barely squeeze our big toes inside one of those now!"

"We'll have to improvise. Rig something bigger, so we both fit."

"And where's the electricity going to come from?"

"Same as last time."

I'm losing patience with this entire conversation. "What's that supposed to mean?"

He shrugs like the answer is obvious.

"Lightning."

CHAPTER TWENTY-SIX

THEO METZINGER

The memory: The minute I wake up, I can tell something is wrong. Headache. Scratchy throat. I throw off the covers and get out of bed. Not dizziness exactly, but a little unsteady for a few seconds.

I check myself. Wrong room. This is Reef's memory, not mine. But, as usual, I'm destined to remember it anyway.

As I (Reef) throw on clothes and head down the long hallway, I start to think about taking a day off school. Nobody could hold it against me. I really am sick—at least I think I am. But school means Portia, and ever since her birthday party, we've been getting close. Inside the memory, I get a sense of the party: lots of kids, music, laughter, food—a great night. No, I'm not too sick. If it means seeing her, I'll tough it out.

Mom is in the small kitchen. The minute I lay eyes on her, I forget about my own head and throat. She looks worse than I feel—very pale, with dark circles under her eyes. Plus she's coughing.

On the way to school, my worry about Mom is replaced by anticipation. I'll see Portia soon. But when I stop by her locker, she isn't there.

She's sick, another friend supplies. "Hope it's not . . ." She leaves the sentence unfinished, but I know what she means. Covid. Everybody thinks it; nobody says it out loud . . .

A frosty blob of milkshake slips down the wrong pipe and I lurch out of the memory, hacking and choking.

From across our table at Fro-Yo Joe's, Portia looks at me in concern. "Brain freeze?"

"Guilty," I confess, but the truth is closer to brain *overload*. The memories have been swirling around my head for a while—all the clues I need to solve the puzzle. But this is the first time I actually put them together.

No wonder Reef is so weird around Portia! The Covid that killed his mom—he got it at *her* party! And he blames himself because he insisted on going over his mother's objections.

"That's why I'm a cone girl," Portia is explaining. "You have to be careful with shakes. If you're thirsty, you'll slurp them down too fast . . ."

All the awful pieces are clicking into place in my mind. Reef never had anything against Portia. He really liked her. But because of what happened, he can't even stand to look at her.

Bad enough to lose your mom. But when the cause of it is something *you* did—that has to be the ultimate torture.

Correction: Reef didn't do anything. This was not his fault; it was *Covid's* fault. Nobody can be sure about anything when it comes to a virus.

But would a grieving, heartbroken kid see it that way?

"Do you know who you got Covid from?" I blurt suddenly.

Portia looks surprised. To her, this is supposed to be a conversation about fro-yo. "I never had Covid."

"But—" I stare at her. "Sure you did. Last year, right after your birthday party. You missed a lot of school."

"Where is this coming from? You didn't even know me then!"

"I overheard some people talking," I say evasively.

"Well, those 'people' are full of it! I didn't have Covid after my birthday. I had mono!"

I'm sure my mouth is hanging open like I'm catching flies.

"Just because there's a pandemic doesn't mean you can't get sick with other things," she informs me. "Mono's awful. I was flat on my back for three weeks."

"I—I—didn't know."

The news is still rattling around my skull as I make my way from Fro-Yo Joe's to Reef's house: Reef's Covid didn't come from Portia's party—and he has no idea. But how can I tell him without admitting that I know through the Phenomenon that he blames himself? That would be rubbing it in his face that I've got a front row seat to his deepest suffering.

He'd never speak to me again, and I can't risk that. Reef and I are hard at work on a plan to escape each other's heads and get our lives back once and for all.

It's tough to be logical and scientific about something that defies logic and science. But there's one thing we agree on: Lightning got us into this, and it's going to take lightning to get us out.

We even know where we're going to get the lightning. Delgado Middle School was built in the 1920s, and it has an old-fashioned lightning rod on top of its cupola. Its purpose is to attract a lightning bolt away from hitting the building and direct it into the ground, where it fizzles out. But if we attach a metal cable to the main rod, some of that electricity can be directed to us.

We've been surfing the internet, researching how to live through a lightning strike. Google says you can't—or at least it's pure luck whether or not you do. But as babies, we weren't struck by lightning either—the hospital was, and our incubator was wired up to the hospital. Incubators are made of acrylic, which doesn't conduct electricity. That's probably why two tiny, fragile infants survived so much high voltage.

Reef closes the browser on his computer. "So we need to be in something made of acrylic?"

"It doesn't have to be acrylic," I reason. "It just has to be a nonconductor. Plastic, rubber—anything but metal."

Reef looks thoughtful. "I wonder what a bouncy castle is made of."

I glare at him. "Be serious."

"I am. The school has one. They set it up for fairs and field days and stuff like that. It's plastic, right?"

I picture any bouncy castle I've ever seen. Not only are they plastic, but they come with an air compressor that keeps them inflated. That way we'd be off the floor and insulated from anything metal. Even better, it's already at the school, so all we'd have to do is drag it up to the cupola and find enough extension cords to plug the compressor in somewhere!

"Reef, you're a genius! The lightning rod sends the electricity to the bouncy castle, where we're insulated—just like we were in the incubator!"

The bedroom door swings open, revealing Declan standing motionless, a stunned expression on his face.

"This is a joke, right?" he says. "Or a project for school where you make a diorama but it isn't something you'd actually *do*?"

Reef and I exchange an agonized glance. We have a decision to make on the fly, and we're not going to have the chance to discuss it: Can we lie our way out of this, or has Declan already heard too much?

"Come on," he persists. "I'm no rat, but I have to tell my folks if that's the only way to keep you guys from getting yourselves killed."

That does it for Reef. "Listen, Declan, this is going to sound pretty weird, but I swear I'm not pulling your chain. Fact is, something's been happening to Theo and me." He goes on to explain about the Phenomenon and how we traced it to that night we were newborns.

It's the first time we've told anybody about our problem and I'm not sure what kind of reaction to expect, especially from Declan, who can be such a jerk. But he listens carefully and waits for Reef to finish before he says anything.

Finally, the verdict comes: "I know you hate me and I know I deserve it. But just how stupid do you think I am?"

“There’s no way we can prove it to you,” I put in evenly. “But do you think we’d be messing with *lightning* if we weren’t desperate?”

It goes back and forth like that for a while, until I actually start to feel a little sorry for Declan. What we’re asking him to accept is pretty out there. But as we keep on describing the Phenomenon—not just the memory swapping, but how confusing it is to live like this, never knowing for sure if your frame of reference comes from your own life or the other guy’s—we begin to get through to him. I show him the notes on my phone, and Reef rolls up his sleeves and pant legs, revealing how he’s turned himself into a human cheat sheet.

I’m not sure if Declan believes what we’re saying, but he’s starting to accept that *we* believe it.

“And the only way to undo this is *lightning*?” he asks in amazement.

“We can’t know if it’ll work,” Reef admits. “But we have to re-create that night in the hospital.”

Declan shakes his head. “I used to lie in bed wishing that something like a lightning bolt would erase you from the face of the earth. But now it feels like I should stop this. It’s not something you let your”—his voice tightens with emotion—“*brother* do.”

“For what it’s worth,” I reply, “I don’t think we’re going to get killed.”

“You’d better not,” Declan says feelingly. “Because if I’m the one helping you, who do you think is going to get blamed when you idiots end up a pair of toasted marshmallows?" We must look stunned, because he adds, "What—you don't think I'm going to let you try this alone, do you?"

It's the first time our plan starts to seem real—the moment when we realize we have a partner.

CHAPTER TWENTY-SEVEN

REEF MOODY

Who knew that checking the weather has more drama than a Marvel movie?

Planning a picnic? You can grow old waiting for a sunny day. But when your whole future rests on lightning, you can barely scrape up a raindrop.

Kids don't normally worry about the forecast, but lately, Theo and I have been glued to the weather apps on our phones and tuned to the Weather Channel 24-7. Can't be sure that redirecting a lightning strike into Delgado's bouncy castle will undo the Phenomenon, but there's definitely a *chance.*

Zero lightning means zero chance.

The only person more weather-obsessed than Theo and me has got to be Declan. Maybe because he's been such a jerk to me for the past year, he's determined to make up for it by being the best partner anybody ever had.

"Reef." One morning, I awaken to him shaking me.

"What time is it?" I mumble. There's no light sneaking in through the blinds.

"It's five thirty. But look." He waves his phone in my face. "There's a forty percent chance of rain at two p.m."

"Rain isn't lightning," I remind him with a yawn.

"It could turn into it."

"Even if it does, at two o'clock, the school is full of kids and teachers. I can just see us cutting class to drag a bouncy castle up to the roof in a building full of people. And what about Theo? At two o'clock, he's halfway across town at his own school."

"Go back to sleep," Declan mumbles resentfully, like I'm the one who's ruining everything.

An hour later, he has me awake again. "Look—they've moved the rain from two to five. Nobody's in school then. And Theo will be at Neighborhood Harvest. That's not too far away."

I have to admit he has a point. But as the day goes on, the chance of rain drops from forty percent to thirty, and later gets downgraded to "slight." Around six, the sun pokes out from behind the clouds. It beams in through the dining room window at the Helmer house.

"It turned out to be a beautiful day after all," Willis comments as we're having dinner.

Declan slams down his water glass and storms away from the table.

"What's up with him?" Liam wants to know.

"He said something about getting an early start on his homework," I say.

"I think that's great," Jenna approves. "It's about time Dec took more of an interest in his education."

Poor Jenna. If she knew what Declan was really interested in, she'd do a backflip.

For the next three days, a high-pressure system passes overhead. You've never seen such blue skies.

Declan takes it personally. "Aw, come on! Is a little bad weather too much to ask for? What happened to the thunderstorms? Aren't they a thing anymore?"

Even Theo is becoming impatient. "If Ben Franklin had to wait this long for lightning, we'd all be using gas lamps," he tells me over the phone.

Then, finally, we get our first glimmer of hope in a single-word broadcast over the Weather Channel: "unsettled."

"Unsettled?" Declan echoes. "What's that supposed to mean?"

Our answer comes with the five-day forecast. On Saturday night, thundershowers are expected to pass over the city.

As it turns out, Theo is watching the Weather Channel too. My phone pings: *SATURDAY NIGHT!!!!*

The plan is on.

Saturday is dreary and overcast, with cold drizzle falling on and off all day.

Declan spends the afternoon hanging out the bedroom

window, arm outstretched, palm up. "What kind of storm is this?" he complains, scowling at the clouds. "Get with it, will you?"

"It's fine," I soothe, checking the forecast on my phone for at least the twentieth time. "The lightning isn't supposed to start till eight. We don't need it now. Plus it'll be easier to sneak into the school when it's dark."

Theo is supposed to come over as soon as he finishes his shift at Neighborhood Harvest, but he's running late. Declan is nervous about that too, and I have to stop him from running over to the food bank to see what the holdup is. I never knew Declan was such a worrywart.

I'm pretty nervous myself, but in my case, it has nothing to do with the possibility that Theo might be a no-show. It says on the internet that the average lightning bolt packs a wallop of three hundred million volts of electricity. I'm about to take that on, with nothing for protection but an inflatable carnival attraction people put their preschoolers on. Yeah, I'm scared.

Theo finally turns up around six thirty, soaked and chastened. "I got lost," he admits. "I forgot your street, and I didn't want to check the notes on my phone because it was raining too hard."

"My bad," I tell him. "I've been having a lot of biking memories lately. I should have known they were coming from you."

"Did you hear any thunder?" Declan probes.

"No, but the weather's closing in," Theo replies. "It's definitely going to get stormy."

We get a ride from Willis—not to the school, but to the

Breezeway Multiplex. The theater is no closer to Delgado than home, but we're stuck with it. Our excuse for tonight is that we're going to a movie, and Willis doesn't want us walking in the rain. He and Jenna are so thrilled that Declan and I get along now that they would have driven us to New York to see a Broadway show.

Willis drops us at the theater and we double back toward the school. By now the rain has picked up, and we're drenched and chilled to the bone. In the distance, thunder rumbles, which means there's definitely lightning somewhere. We pick up our pace to a jog.

At Delgado, we find the parking lot deserted, which means there are no custodians in the building. That's good news in a way—we don't have to worry about getting caught. But it also means the school is locked up tight.

That doesn't bother Declan. It doesn't even slow him down. He leads us around the building, tapping and poking every window within reach. Eventually, he finds one unlocked—the girls' changing room next to the gym. We boost him inside and in a few short minutes, a fire door swings wide to reveal Declan, smiling and beckoning.

Once inside, our next order of business is the bouncy castle, which is kept in the storeroom next to the athletic director's office. It probably hasn't been used in a while, because it's one hundred percent deflated and buried under every football, baseball, basketball, soccer ball, tetherball, badminton racket, lacrosse stick, field hockey stick, and volleyball net the school owns.

It's a major operation. We start by shoving all the other

stuff into the four corners of the room. Then we gather up the miles of bright yellow vinyl material that make up the bouncy castle.

"I didn't think it would be so heavy," Theo pants, piling fold after fold over his shoulder.

It's all connected by a plastic corrugated tube to a compressor about the size of an extra-large suitcase. Its job is to pump up the castle and keep it inflated in spite of all the bouncing that's going on. Tonight, we won't be doing any bouncing, but we still need the compressor to keep the castle full under our weight.

Theo and I manage to get hold of all the material that will fill with air and become the vinyl structure. Declan hefts the compressor.

"Thanks for being here, man," I tell him sincerely. "There's no way we could pull this off without you."

Outside, we hear the rumble of thunder. "Let's get up there before we miss all the good lightning," Declan urges.

Delgado has an elevator, but you need a key to operate it. So we have to drag the bouncy castle and compressor up the flight of steps to the second floor and halfway across the building to the upstairs maintenance office. There, amid the industrial vacuums, floor polishers, and cleaning supplies, is the roof access—a thin metal circular stairway. Getting everything up these narrow, steep steps is like trying to cram a golf ball through a straw. It takes all three of us, grunting, gasping, and sweating, to inch up those stairs, struggling to keep the piles of vinyl from getting away from us.

At the very top, there's a trapdoor. I have to open it with one hand to avoid dropping my share of the bouncy castle and wiping out Theo and Declan. I open the hatch on its hinges and climb up a short ladder to the cupola on the roof.

The cupola looks gigantic from the street, but there's really not that much room here. It's round and about the size of a very small bedroom. A decorative roof overhead offers some protection, but gusty rain is blowing in through the open sides, soaking a mix of gravel, dirt, and dead leaves. It's pretty obvious that no one's been up here for a long time.

It takes some doing to get first Theo and then Declan to join me in the cupola along with the rest of the bouncy castle and the compressor.

"So this is the cupola," Theo says to me with a goofy grin. "If it wasn't for this place, I never would have been able to track you down through your memories."

"Is the bouncy castle even going to fit?" Declan asks anxiously.

He has a point. Even flat as a pancake, the folds of vinyl castle fill up most of the floor of the structure, so there's barely anywhere for us to stand.

"Only one way to find out," I reply.

There's no electrical outlet in the cupola, so we have to plug in the compressor in the maintenance office below us. Luckily, one thing custodians have a lot of is extension cords. We leave the unit by the trapdoor and hit inflate.

The compressor is loud. I mean really loud—the kind of noise where you have to shout at each other just to be heard.

"I can't hear the storm anymore," Declan protests. "We could be missing a lot of lightning."

I point straight up. "The lightning rod is right on top of that roof. If it gets hit, trust me, we'll know."

Theo takes off his backpack, unzips it, and pulls out six shiny clothes hangers.

Declan stares at him. "What—you want to have a fashion show up here?"

"They're pure copper," Theo explains. "It's the best electrical conductor in the world. We'll open them up and use them to connect the lightning rod to the bouncy castle."

Speaking of the bouncy castle . . . it's starting to take shape all around us and under our feet as the vinyl fills with air from the compressor. As the "turrets" begin to form, they press up against the cupola walls, bending inward toward the domed ceiling.

Theo unwinds the copper hangers and ties them together into a cable. He connects one end to the ground wire leading down from the lightning rod. The other he extends out over the bouncy castle, resting it on one of the walls. The inflatable playhouse is full now, if a little squeezed. The corners of the square base rise up the rounded walls of the cupola. Doesn't look much like the incubator we were confined in twelve and a half years ago, but it should serve the same purpose.

"There," Theo announces when the job is done. "We're ready."

That means there's nothing left for us to do except climb on there and wait to be zapped.

"Take your belts off first," Declan advises. "The buckles are metal, and that could get you toasted."

"Good idea," Theo decides.

We heave ourselves up onto the springy plastic base and toss our belts to Declan.

He hesitates, worried. "What about your jeans? They could have metal studs that conduct electricity."

"If I get killed tonight, I don't want the fire department to find me in my underwear," Theo retorts.

"True that," I add.

Declan's face twists. "Yeah, but *don't* get killed."

I wish I could say something comforting to him, but I can't think of what. I have no reason to expect we'll survive this except for the fact that we did survive it as babies all those years go.

Declan retreats down the spiral ladder, closing the trapdoor behind him. We're alone with the storm.

Theo reclines on the vinyl base, propped up on his elbows. "If this goes bad . . ." He falls silent.

I know what he means. If we're wrong about this and the great-granddaddy of all lightning bolts is about to blast us into oblivion, there won't be time to say goodbye.

"You're a good guy, Basket Case," I mumble around the lump in my throat. And I actually *know* he's a good guy, because a lot of his life is parked in my brain. I was so ticked off about losing my memories of Mom that I never gave Theo a chance. I'm still ticked off. He deserves better than that, even if it comes now, in what might be our final conversation. When you share something so personal as memories with someone, the word *friend* doesn't even come close to describing the connection between you. Even *brother* falls short.

A flash of lightning makes us both jump, and I tense all over, waiting to be fricasseed.

Theo's sheepish smile tells me he did the same. "If you see the flash, it already missed us."

He has a point. That's another thing about Theo. He's smart.

I angle myself on the castle's spongy base so I can peer out the opening in the cupola. I don't see any more lightning, just a few flickers way off in the distance. In fact, I think the rain is starting to slacken.

The trapdoor is thrown open and Declan charges up into the cupola, his face grim.

"Get out of here, Declan!" I shout at him. "It isn't safe!"

He stomps right onto the bouncy castle and peers out at the sky. "What kind of storm is this?" he howls. "Where's my lightning?"

"It might be moving off," Theo offers apologetically.

Declan stretches his arm outside. "It isn't even raining anymore!" He scowls into the night. "You stink! And is that a star? *No-o!*"

It's not just a star; it's a lot of stars. The sky is beginning to clear.

I can't even describe the strange mix of emotions running through me. Relief, sure—I can't hide it, even from myself. No one *wants* to get zapped with three hundred million volts.

But my *reason* for getting zapped hasn't gone away. I still have a head full of the wrong memories, and the *right* memories are someplace else. We're back where we started. Actually, it's worse than that. We have to deflate the bouncy castle and drag it down to the storeroom to get to zero—all while knowing that we're going to have to go through this again and again until it either works, or we get killed.

Declan is still shaking his fist at the heavens. "You call that a thunderstorm? Oh, please! The forecasters in this town are morons!"

Theo scoots down the ladder and turns off the compressor. Even Declan interrupts his ranting to help us stomp the air out of the bouncy castle. It takes a long time and we don't get all of it, so wrestling the monster back to the main floor is even harder than bringing it upstairs. We hide the cable of copper hangers under a pile of sports equipment in the storeroom.

When at last we're done, standing in the parking lot, exhausted and dripping sweat, Willis texts from the movie theater. He's there to pick us up. Where are we?

Declan calls his dad. "We figured you wanted us to walk home, since it isn't raining anymore. And there's no lightning. That part's definite."

"At least you guys are almost home," Theo comments wearily. "I still have to bike halfway across town."

I honestly never thought of that. Then again, when you're expecting to take a direct hit from a lightning bolt, you don't make plans for later that night.

"You can sleep over," Declan decides. "We'll work on our strategy for next time."

Next time! Theo and I exchange a look of pure agony.

It took a lot to get us into that cupola tonight.

How are we ever going to work up the courage to do it again?

CHAPTER TWENTY-EIGHT

THEO METZINGER

We're back to watching the Weather Channel, cheering on tropical depressions and booing sunny skies. For days, we follow a line of thunderstorms across the country, anticipating its approach, yet also dreading it. All too well we remember how it felt to sit in the rain-swept cupola, waiting for a bolt of lightning to set us free, but also maybe kill us.

"These storms mess with your head!" Declan complains. "They get your hopes up and then they waste all the good stuff on other towns! In Asheville, two people and a chinchilla got struck by lightning—and they didn't even need it!"

"At least they survived," Reef points out. "That proves it's *possible*."

"Those jerks are hogging all the good lightning" is Declan's opinion.

Now that the front is approaching us, it's barely scattered showers.

"The forecaster said it could strengthen again," I offer.

We have a decision to make. In a few hours, the weather system will be here. Do we go back to the cupola and try it all over again? Or do we wait for a storm that promises more than a few raindrops?

We waffle back and forth, and, at the last minute, we decided to sit this one out. It's no small thing to break into the school and drag the bouncy castle and compressor all the way to the roof. Plus it takes a lot for Reef and me to psych ourselves up to risk our lives again. We're determined to reverse the Phenomenon, but that doesn't mean it still isn't plenty terrifying.

That night, thunder booms and lightning forks across the sky for three harrowing hours.

Declan is sullen. "The Weather Channel should be forced off the air for this! Light rain, my butt!"

I hear him raving in the background when I call Reef in the middle of it.

"He's got a point," Reef tells me. "This storm is pretty intense, and it doesn't seem to be ending. Maybe we should try to get up to the cupola fast."

"It's too late," I tell him. "It takes me forty-five minutes to get there on a good day. And how am I supposed to explain to my parents that I'm taking my bike out in the middle of the night when it's thundering and raining cats and dogs? Face it—we missed this one."

I don't add what he probably already suspects—that my memory is so mixed up with his that I can't trust myself to find Breezeway in the dark. These days, I'm navigating purely by phone, something I can't do in a downpour.

We have no choice but to wait for the next storm. A new tropical depression coming up from Florida is expected to collide with a low-pressure system moving across the country next Tuesday or Wednesday. Nobody knows all the details yet, but the forecasters agree on one thing: It's going to be big.

"This is it!" Declan exclaims on the phone. "If you guys can't get struck by lightning in *this*, then you're not trying!" He lets out a little gulp, which means his mind has caught up with his mouth, and he's thinking about what we have to do.

"You're watching *weather* again?" My father can't believe it. "Really, Theo? That's the best you can do with your free time? When I was your age, I used to—"

"Rule the school," I finish. "Yeah, Dad, you mentioned it. Weather is awesome."

Maybe too awesome. The forecast starts to fall into place: The first bands of rain will arrive late Tuesday afternoon, and by dinnertime, it should be in full swing. Cloudbursts. Wind gusts. Lightning. It's not going to be fun to be up on that roof, but one thing is certain: We'll get our chance to reverse the Phenomenon. This might be the best chance we ever get.

Even Declan is upbeat about Tuesday. *Nothing can stop us this time!!!* he texts.

On Monday, when I ride up to Delgado to meet Portia and walk over to Neighborhood Harvest, the words are spelled out in block capitals on the sign on the front lawn:

OPEN SCHOOL NIGHT—TUESDAY 7 P.M.

"Are you okay, Theo?" Portia asks in concern. "All the color is gone from your face."

I point. "What's that?"

"Open School Night? We have that every year. Kids bring their families. Teachers open up their classrooms, and there's food and games—it's really fun."

"Yeah, but it's small, right?" I manage weakly. "I mean, things like this are big in elementary, but once you get to middle school, nobody shows up for that kind of stuff."

Portia laughs. "You must be kidding. At Delgado, nobody misses Open School Night. We even get out-of-towners—grandparents, aunts and uncles. It's huge. I'm on the planning committee. I was going to ask if you want to come tomorrow, but you probably can't bike. It's supposed to rain."

"I *might* come."

Who am I kidding? Of course I'm going to be there. That's not the problem! I picture the major operation of dragging the bouncy castle up to the roof. I think about the roar of the compressor. Now I picture the school packed with people, the parking lot jammed with cars.

We had a plan . . . up until two minutes ago. But how are we going to make this work in the middle of Open School Night? I turn it over every which way in my mind, but I just can't find a solution. You can't sneak unnoticed through a crowd carrying a deflated bouncy castle and its compressor.

But we can't pass up this storm. If we let winter settle in, we might not see lightning again for months.

Reef and I can't wait that long.

CHAPTER TWENTY-NINE

REEF MOODY

"Open School Night!" I slam my fist into my pillow. "How could I forget about that?"

"The same way we've both been forgetting everything else." Theo tries to soothe me.

"Yeah? So why didn't *you* remember it?"

"Maybe I did. But when you get a memory that isn't yours, you've got no idea how important it is. For all I knew, that sign was from years ago."

Theo is playing hooky from Neighborhood Harvest. The minute he found out about Open School Night, he blew off Portia and biked straight here to share the bad news.

Perched on the edge of Declan's desk, Theo shifts his weight. "Maybe we can work Open School Night to our advantage."

"What advantage?" I snap. "You're going to ask Latimore to carry the bouncy castle for us? And the compressor can fit in her belly button?"

"Last time, the school was locked up tight," Theo reasons. "Tomorrow night, we can just waltz right in with everybody else."

"And the crowd?" I challenge.

"We're thinking of them as an obstacle," he explains. "We

can use them as cover. We'll blend right in—especially you and Declan. It's your school. If people see us carrying a giant thing, they'll assume we're helping out. And we'll stay in the middle of the pack so the teachers don't see us with something we're not supposed to have."

"We'll never pull it off," I predict mournfully.

But Theo is growing animated as he gets into the details of how all this can work. "I know someone on the planning committee for Open School Night. I bet I can get us badges or T-shirts that say we're working for the school. Come to think of it, it might be a good idea to have an insider helping us out."

"What insider?" I demand, although I already know the answer.

"Portia."

"Forget it," I say firmly.

"Why?"

"We've talked about this fifty times!" I explode. "The Phenomenon isn't normal. I don't want to blab about it to everybody so they'll think we've lost our minds!"

"We told Declan and the world didn't end. Portia's just one more person. We *need* more help—especially from someone on the committee who knows exactly how Open School Night is going to be set up."

"You're just trying to get your girlfriend in on this," I accuse him.

"She's not my girlfriend!"

"Aren't you forgetting something?" I smirk. "I've got your memories. I know exactly how you feel about Portia!"

"Yeah, well, I've got your memories too!" he retorts. "So I know you don't care if she's my girlfriend or not. Why don't you admit the real reason you're so dead set against Portia helping us?"

"Because—" I can't tell him. I can't tell anybody. I've never said it out loud—not even in a dark room when I'm all alone. "Because—" I try to form the words, but they just don't come.

Then Theo says, "Portia didn't kill your mother."

It's all I can do to keep from throwing myself at him, fists flying. The fury that courses through me isn't so much because of what he said. It's that he had the courage to say it and I didn't.

"Don't you think I know that?" I seethe. "Portia didn't get my mom sick. *I* did—with the Covid I brought home from *her* birthday party!"

"That's the thing," Theo insists. "Portia never had Covid."

"You don't know what you're talking about! You weren't even around then! She was out of school for weeks!"

"Yeah—with *mono*! There was no Covid at Portia's party. You didn't get it from there, which means you couldn't have given it to your mom. Who knows where it came from?"

I just stare at him, my mouth hanging open.

"It's true," he adds in a quiet voice. "I wanted to tell you sooner, but the time never seemed right. I know you hate talking about what happened."

It's like I've been hit over the head and I'm struggling to fight my way back to consciousness. This is something I've believed for so long—thinking about it, beating myself up over it, every day, every hour, practically every minute. To suddenly find out it's not true makes me dizzy. I nagged Mom into letting me go to the party and the two of us got sick at the same time Portia did. It seemed so obvious: I got it from Portia and gave it to my mother.

But *Portia never had Covid*!

There are a dozen ways the virus could have gotten to us. Mom worked in a busy bank; I went to a busy school. It wasn't anybody's fault. Covid was everywhere, spreading like wildfire. It found us the same way it found millions of people.

I can't describe the feeling. This doesn't change anything. Mom is still gone. But it wasn't the party. It wasn't *me*. It's like the guilt that's been pressing down on me—the weight of a thousand planets—turns to helium and just sort of floats away.

Nothing is different except everything.

Theo is regarding me intently. "You okay, Reef?"

I nod. I *am* okay . . . better than okay. But I don't dare say that out loud for fear that it all might pop like a soap bubble. Is this real? How can it be real?

I look to Theo for confirmation.

He's one thousand percent serious. "So we talk to Portia?"

I nod again.

I walk by Fro-Yo Joe's every day, but I haven't been inside since Mom died. That's where we take Portia to explain the unexplainable.

We pick her and Declan up at Neighborhood Harvest. If Portia tries to say, "No one would ever believe a nutty story like that," we've got Declan as proof that somebody did.

Obviously, the hardest part for any newcomer to accept is the Phenomenon. At first, she thinks we're kidding. Then she gets mad—like we're trying to make a fool of her. But when it starts to sink in that we believe what we're saying, she becomes alarmed.

"This is not possible. Things like this can't happen!"

Declan jumps in to support us. "Do you think they'd be desperate enough to get struck by lightning if it wasn't real?"

She's wide-eyed, yogurt dripping down her chin. "Okay, that part's not true for sure!"

So we explain the history of the two newborns in the incubator.

She's sputtering now. "And you think being *electrocuted*—making it happen again—is going to undo everything? First of all: *No*. And second: Are you both *trying* to get killed?"

"They might not get killed," Declan argues. "People survive lightning every day. You know—people and chinchillas."

Portia goggles at him.

"That's where the bouncy castle comes in," Theo explains reasonably. "It'll insulate us—just like the incubator did when we were babies."

She turns pleading eyes to me. "And you think this makes sense?"

I'm honest. "We can't go on like this." I pull up my sleeves, revealing the survival notes scribbled up and down both arms.

"This is what it takes to get me through a normal day, and even then, I sometimes forget what class to go to, or how to find my own house. My grades are tanking because I can't remember things anymore. And . . . I've lost my memories of my mother. Her face, the sound of her voice. She's just—gone."

"Oh, Reef!" She reaches out for both my hands. I remember the last time that happened. We were saying good night as I left her party to go home to the apartment I shared with Mom.

"So you'll help us?" Theo presses.

"For all the good it'll do," she replies, her voice raspy with emotion. "I have to try to keep you two from getting electrocuted. Man, I hope you know what you're doing!"

An uneasy glance passes between Theo and me.

We hope so too.

CHAPTER THIRTY

THEO METZINGER

The confusion always hits hardest in the morning. My life; Reef's life. My house; the Helmer home; Reef's apartment. I feel the effects in small ways. The medicine cabinet opens the wrong way and whacks me on the side of the head. The staircase has one more step and I nearly twist my ankle. The cereal bowl is too big and I drown my Honey Nut Cheerios.

I shrug into my backpack and head out to the garage for my bike. On the front walk, I spy Jaws in the flower bed, helping himself to a couple of marigolds. I start to shoo him away, but something holds me back.

I am about to take on the full power of nature. What will happen is impossible to predict. Our plan could work . . . or maybe it won't. We might even spend another couple of hours in the cupola waiting for a lightning strike that isn't coming. But there's also a chance—I can't know how big—that Reef and I both get electrocuted tonight. Which means this could be the last time I ever see this rabbit, who has become a part of my life.

Cautiously, I approach. Jaws turns from his snack and watches me with suspicion.

"It's okay, little guy," I tell him. "I'm not going to chase you."

Jaws doesn't believe me. The rabbit bounds away and scoots. I guess it's Reef who's earned his trust, not me. I shouldn't care, but somehow I do.

Horn honking, Dad pulls into the driveway, screeching to a halt inches from the garage door. He leaps out and hits the path running. "Forgot something!" He disappears and is back in a few seconds, carrying a computer bag. "Hop in, Theo," he offers. "I'll give you a lift."

"That's okay, Dad," I reply. "I'm taking my bike. Reef and I are meeting after school."

He smiles at me and I can almost see a hint of the prideful affection that he usually saves for my sister. "Busy man—places to go, people to see. Couple of months ago, your best friends were plants."

"I still like gardening," I tell him stubbornly.

"Nothing wrong with that. But you're an athlete now. You grew shoulders. You're living the life."

Living the life. I know he means it as a compliment—it's almost as good as ruling the school. But it occurs to me then that everything I thought about Jaws also goes for Dad. This might be the last conversation I ever have with my father.

Next thing I know, I'm throwing my arms around him and hugging him tight.

"Whoa!" he exclaims. "What brought that on?"

"Nothing," I mumble. "Have a great day, Dad."

"Yeah, you too, Theo." He gets into the car, but stops at the end of the driveway and rolls down his window. "Careful on the bike. I think it might storm later."

"Really?" I gulp. "I haven't checked the weather."

I take my time riding to Breezeway at three thirty. Open School Night doesn't start until seven, so there's no ticking clock. Also, we can't do anything until the lightning starts, and so far, there isn't a cloud in the sky. If the storm of the century is really coming, it's counting on the element of surprise.

By the time I get to the Helmer house, Reef and Declan have already been home almost an hour. Reef has three T-shirts for us, smuggled via Portia. They're bright blue—school colors—with the message: LEARNING IS A DELGADO ADVENTURE.

Declan makes a face when he sees them. "Why do schools always say 'learning' like it's something to be proud of? Don't they know most kids run a mile when they hear that word?"

"This is what the student volunteers are going to be wearing tonight," Reef explains. "If we're in these shirts, nobody will ask any questions, like 'Where are you going with that bouncy castle?'"

I shrug into my T-shirt. "It's all good." Or at least as good as it can be when you're about to play patty-cake with a thunderbolt.

"Good?" Declan echoes. "Look at that blue sky! How are we supposed to get lightning out of that? The only thing missing is a palm tree and a tiki hut!"

"The weather forecast hasn't changed," I insist. "It's coming. My dad even warned me to be careful on my bike because it's going to get stormy."

Jenna makes us an early dinner of sandwiches and potato chips, since we're going to be "on duty" at the school. She's pretty thrilled about that, and takes dozens of pictures of us in our "Learning" T-shirts.

"Cut it out, Mom," Declan barks. "I wouldn't be caught dead in this thing. I'm only wearing it because . . ." His voice trails off.

"Because you have such great school spirit," Reef finishes the sentence for him.

Jenna isn't quite sure how I fit in, but she treats me like I'm part of the family. Maybe she thinks I'm the reason Reef and her son Declan are getting along so well now.

We're back upstairs when Portia calls me. She's at Delgado already, helping to set up for Open School Night. There are a lot of voices in the background, and plenty of noise, so it's hard to hear her.

"Theo, this is important. We've got a problem."

"What problem?" I ask anxiously.

"It's not good," she informs me. "Listen—"

The strident voice of a teacher breaks in. "Portia, get off the phone! We need your help here!"

"Call me back," I request urgently.

"I don't know if I can," she replies. "My phone is at three percent."

"Portia!" the teacher exclaims.

With a click, Portia's gone.

"Problem?" That's the one word Declan took from the conversation. "What problem?"

"She couldn't say," I report. "Some teacher needed her. She's going to try to call back, but her phone is dying."

We wait—ten minutes, then twenty. No Portia. I try her number. Straight to voice mail.

"And this girl gets straight As?" Declan raves. "What's the point of being smart if you don't know enough to charge your phone when you've got a long night coming up?"

"Maybe it's no big deal," Reef muses.

"She said *problem*," I reason. "That's never great. Maybe we should head over there."

"In these shirts?" Declan is horrified. "They'll make us work!"

We hang around another ten minutes, hoping that Portia can borrow someone else's phone and let us know what we're up against. Nothing. Finally, we've got no choice but to go to Delgado, find Portia, and face our "problem," whatever it is.

Before we leave, Jenna makes us pose for more pictures. I guess when your kid is Declan, and he's doing something at his school that isn't stealing the principal's pocketbook, you want to capture the moment forever.

"Enough, Mom!" he grouses, heading out the door.

But Reef lingers around Jenna. I think he's feeling what I felt leaving my own home—that maybe he won't be back. Jenna may not be his mother, but she sure came up big for him when he needed it.

The sky is still clear during our walk to school, and Declan is convinced that Portia's call was to warn us that we won't be getting our storm.

"Yes, we will," I insist.

But even I'm starting to wonder. You can't have a storm without at least a few clouds, and there just aren't any. We're only a block from school when a gray weather front appears on the horizon. Once it's there, though, it races across the sky, blotting out the sun. A stiff breeze comes up from the west, sending leaves and dust swirling. Thirty feet from the front entrance, we feel the first raindrops.

"It's about time!" Declan growls at the heavens.

Be careful what you wish for. As if on cue, a sudden drenching rain comes down in sheets. We barely manage to scramble indoors before getting soaked.

Delgado's halls are already pretty crowded. I'm surprised by how many parents, grandparents, and siblings are here. Portia's right—Open School Night is a big deal. The corridors echo with laughter and animated conversation and the rapid-fire putt-putt-putt of a motor that's strangely familiar.

The double doors of the gym are propped open, revealing the bouncy castle in all its bright yellow glory. Little kids are climbing, jumping, sliding, and scrambling around to join the end of the line to climb, jump, and slide again.

Declan is outraged. "That's *our* bouncy castle!"

"They knew they'd get families," I reason. "It makes perfect sense that they'd set it up for the younger sibs."

"Just our luck!" Declan laments. "How are we going to drag that thing up to the roof when it's full of kids?"

I'm trying to stay calm. "Well, obviously, we're going to have to find a substitute."

At that moment, Portia comes up behind us, wide-eyed and breathing hard. "Sorry, my phone died. What are we going to do?"

"Any chance the school has a backup bouncy castle?" I'm joking, but nobody laughs, not even me.

"Can we try it without the bouncy castle?" Reef suggests.

"Only if we want to get burned to a crisp," I reply grimly. "Surely there's something else we can drag up there—something that isn't metal that will fit inside the cupola."

The answer comes from, of all people, Declan. "My science class did a space unit where we went into this black tent and there were stars on the ceiling."

"The planetarium!" Reef exclaims in a hushed voice. "That'll fit, won't it?"

"I think they keep it in the storeroom in the science wing," Portia says. "Follow me."

She leads us through the crowded corridors up the stairs to the science hall on the second floor. I like Portia a lot, but when you're trying to avoid attracting attention, she's just about the worst guide anybody could ever have. She's friends with basically everybody, and no one can seem to pass her by without checking in. I get a lot of strange looks and keep my head down to avoid having to explain who I am and what I'm doing there in a Delgado T-shirt.

There are two science labs, and both are full of people watching students performing chemistry and physics demonstrations. The storeroom sits between the two. We barge in, hoping our T-shirts make it look like we're on official Open School Night business.

The planetarium has been struck down and packed away in a carrying case about the size of a large backpack. I throw it over my shoulder and then we venture out into the Open School Night crowd again, with Portia greeting the same friends, this time heading in the opposite direction.

As we slip through the door into the upstairs maintenance office, I know a moment of uncertainty. It would only take one custodian to throw a monkey wrench into this entire operation. Four sighs of relief sound as the door closes behind us. We're alone. All the maintenance staff are on duty throughout the building. When the school is filled with hundreds of visitors, nobody worries about what's happening on the roof.

The packed planetarium is a lot easier to handle than the bouncy castle and compressor—which turns out to be a good news–bad news kind of thing. Up in the blowing wind and rain of the cupola, we open the backpack only to find a pile of plastic tentpoles and miles of thick black fabric. An instruction sheet declares: DELUXE PLANETARIUM—SOME ASSEMBLY REQUIRED.

"*Some* assembly?" Declan rages into the storm. "*Some?* What kind of cheapo school buys a rip-off planetarium from Ikea?"

"Let's just build it," Reef says through clenched teeth. "What choice do we have?"

We have to insert the poles into the fabric while the howling wind threatens to hurl the whole business off the roof, us included. It isn't heavy, but it's a strenuous job, since you have to hang on to the fabric and position the poles, while at the same time stepping on the base to keep it from flying away. All this while taking a faceful of battering rain.

While we're working, I catch a very recent memory from Reef from just a few minutes ago—planetarium construction from a different angle: *This isn't worth it.*

"Yes, it is," I tell him, and he knows exactly what I mean.

When we're finally finished, a new problem emerges. Unlike the inflatable bouncy castle, the base of this planetarium is a thin sheet of vinyl. There's no way it's enough insulation to protect us from a lightning strike.

"You mean we can't use it?" Declan shrills in horror. "After all our hard work?"

"We need thicker protection under us," I insist. "Something plastic or rubber maybe."

"How about the gymnastics mats from PE?" Reef suggests. "We could stack a few on the floor of the tent."

Portia shakes her head. "Too risky. Those mats are held together by metal staples that might conduct electricity. We need something that's pure nonconductor, like rubber tires."

Declan is sarcastic. "Oh, no problem, then! Don't all middle schools keep whole storerooms of tires just in case somebody needs to get struck by lightning?"

"The playground!" Reef exclaims excitedly. "The tire

swing has a giant truck tire that's big enough for two people to sit on!"

Our missions are set: Reef, Declan, and I will head out to the playground for the tire, while Portia ventures down to the gym storeroom to recover the chain of copper hangers to connect us to the lightning rod. Before exiting the maintenance office, I pull a hacksaw off a rack of tools and hide it under my shirt.

Outside, the rain has slackened a little, but the lightning has begun. I take a moment to count the seconds between each flash and the clap of thunder that follows. *One . . . two . . . three . . . four . . .* That means the center of the storm is only four miles away. We don't have much time.

At the playground, the tire swing hangs in the center of the jungle gym, suspended via three stout ropes. I cut through the ropes with the hacksaw, and the heavy wheel thumps to the sand.

It takes all our strength to pick the tire off the ground, but once we stand it upright, we can roll it. That's what we do—we maneuver it across the schoolyard like a giant hoop, and direct it into the building, entering via a side stairwell. Then comes the hard part, dragging it up the steps. Declan and I push from behind, with Reef in front, stabilizing and guiding. The three of us know that if we ever lose control of this thing, Declan and I will end up at the bottom of the stairs, flat as pancakes.

By this time, Open School Night is in full swing, and

we attract a lot of attention rolling a giant wet tire down the second-floor hall.

"Excuse me," Reef says, directing people out of our way. "School project coming through." The crowd parts to let us pass.

Declan is impressed. "Adults are such idiots! All you have to say is 'school project' and they'll let you get away with anything! You could bring a nuclear warhead in here and nobody would give you a hard time!"

He insists on switching places with Reef, so he can take the lead, chirping the magic words, "Make way for the school project . . . Serious students here . . . Learning is a Delgado adventure . . . Yikes!"

The tire comes to an abrupt halt, and I rear-end it with my face. I've never met Principal Latimore before, but I recognize her immediately via Reef's memories. She's tall and slender, and when she talks to you, it's from a great height because she wears five-inch stiletto heels. I duck behind the tire so she won't see a non-student wearing a Delgado T-shirt and ask too many nosy questions I have no answers for.

"It's wonderful to see you taking an interest in school activities, Declan," she declares. "What's the project? What are you studying?"

Declan has absolutely no idea. All he can stammer is, "Uh—tires?"

Reef steps forward. "It's for the electricity demonstration in the science lab. You know—how rubber is the best insulator?"

She beams. "Very good. I hope you have a successful demonstration."

"Us too," Declan tells her.

Amen, I add silently. If this "demonstration" is *un*successful, I don't want to think about what it means for Reef and me.

When the principal clicks away, we roll the tire into the upstairs maintenance office and slam the door.

Portia is waiting for us, holding on to the string of bent copper hangers. "What took you guys so long?"

"You try dragging a humongous tire all over the place," Declan retorts. "We just ran into Latimore out there. We got away with it, but that's not going to last when she looks at the playground tomorrow and wonders why there's no tire swing."

It takes all four of us, with much effort and grunting, to roll the heavy tire around the circular stairs to the open air of the cupola. A loud clap of thunder makes us jump, and we very nearly lose control of the tire. But we manage to shove it up the final steps into the well of the cupola. Portia holds open the flap of the planetarium, and we heave the tire inside. When the heavy rubber hits bottom, it shakes the wooden structure—or maybe it's the thunder, which is still echoing around us.

"The storm must be really close," Reef comments in a small voice.

I attach one end of the cable of hangers to the lightning rod and stretch the other in through the flap, resting it on the tire.

Portia looks torn. "I know it's what we worked for, but are you guys sure you want to go through with this?"

Reef and I share a meaningful glance. Portia's new to the Phenomenon, but the two of us have been living it for months. Do we want to? Absolutely not. Do we have to? Nothing has ever been so certain.

"Let's do it," I tell her.

Declan's face is pale, and he nods as if to convince himself it's the only way.

Reef and I are about to crawl into the planetarium when the sound reaches us. It's faint amid the howl of the wind and the rumble of thunder, but there's no mistaking it—a door slamming below us.

"Hide!" hisses Declan.

It could not be more obvious that there's nowhere to hide. There's only the planetarium . . . and that's no place to be unless you're trying to get struck by lightning.

Filled with dread, the four of us stand there, waiting for the vibration of footfalls on the metal of the circular stairs. It doesn't come. I tiptoe down the cupola steps and peer through the open trapdoor. Nobody's there.

"Maybe it was a car door out in the parking lot," I offer with a shrug.

A fork of lightning is followed instantly by a deafening boom. The storm is right overhead. It's now or never.

Declan and Portia move closer, and it seems like we're in for some kind of emotional farewell. After all, this goodbye might be permanent.

Please don't let me cry, I exhort myself. The thought brings on a brief snapshot from Reef's funeral memories. I'm grateful that I'm the one forced to see it, not him. This moment is tough enough.

Then it's over. Reef and I climb into the planetarium and perch on the giant tire. For better or worse, this is happening. We're newborns again, huddled together in our incubator.

Declan and Portia stand there, peering in at us like we're a museum exhibit they've waited a lifetime to see.

"Go!" Reef snaps at them. "Get downstairs, away from here!"

Still they stay, until another thunderclap sends them scurrying.

The wind ruffles the tent fabric, moving the cable of copper hangers a little closer to me. Instinctively, I shuffle away from it along the tire, as if another few inches might make a difference when there are three hundred million volts surging through that thing.

Through the flap, I watch Declan and Portia disappear into the trapdoor to the maintenance office below.

"At least they're safe," I tell Reef.

My words hang in the air. You definitely can't say that about us.

The next thing I know, Declan and Portia are climbing up to the roof again, followed by a third figure. I crawl forward on the tire for a better view, but my arm makes contact with the hangers and I jump back like I've been burned.

"Latimore . . ." Reef breathes.

Delgado's principal is in a towering rage. "Have you lost your minds?" she demands. "What on *earth* are you doing with our planetarium in the middle of this storm? Why are you on the roof at all?"

Declan starts babbling about a school project since that's what worked before. The principal silences him with a scorching look.

Her furious gaze shifts to me. "Who are you? You're not one of my students!"

"I'm Theo—"

Reef's voice is shaking, but his determination never wavers. "Sorry, Principal Latimore, but we *have* to do this. You can suspend us tomorrow, even expel us—"

For the first time, the principal notices the truck tire we're sitting on and puts two and two together—our "school project" for the electricity demonstration and ". . . rubber is the best insulator."

"Get out of there! *Now!*" She stalks forward, reaching into the planetarium to pull us out. Her arm brushes against the line of hangers.

"Get back!" Declan lunges at her, shoving her away from the copper cable.

Unsteady on her spiked heels, the principal loses her balance and goes down. Declan trips over her and the two of them end up on the cupola floor.

The flash comes from everywhere at the same time, along with a boom so deafening that it cancels all other sound. A blinding point of light sizzles from the lightning rod to the hangers.

I feel a devastating jolt to every single cell of my body at the same time.

The world goes dark.

CHAPTER THIRTY-ONE

REEF MOODY

The first thing I remember is blinking.

The light is blinding, overpowering, and I can't keep my eyes open for more than a split second.

"Reef?" comes a voice I don't recognize.

That's right! I'm Reef! And along with that thought comes a wave of other information. The cupola. The *lightning*! Surely that was lightning! What else could it have been? Once, when I was in kindergarten, I stuck my finger in a lamp socket while my teacher was changing the bulb. It felt like that times a gazillion. Or did that happen to Theo—

Theo. Is he all right? If I got zapped, so did he!

"Can you hear me, Reef?" that same voice persists.

With effort, I strain to keep my blinking eyelids open a little longer. No wonder it's so bright. Someone is shining a flashlight into my eyes. I duck out of its path and see a white-coated man with a stethoscope around his neck.

I got struck by lightning! I try to say the words. I can almost hear them. But they don't come out of my mouth.

My eyes are open now, and I can see that I'm in a hospital bed, hooked up to IV bags and monitors. My shoulder is bandaged three-quarters of the way to my wrist. Funny, it didn't hurt before, but now that I know it's bandaged, waves of pain radiate up and down my arm. Come to think of it, everything hurts. My head pounds, my jaw is sore, and muscle aches extend from my neck down to the tips of my toes.

"Are you able to speak?" the doctor asks urgently.

I'm trying to! I want to scream. Why can't I say anything? Did the lightning burn off my tongue? No, it's definitely still there. I wiggle it around my mouth, and finally, my first words tumble out.

"Where's Theo?"

He looks pleased. "Very good," he approves, making notes on a clipboard.

"Where's Theo?" I demand, surprised at how hostile my tone is.

He seems taken aback for a moment, and then chuckles. "I see you're going to be fine. Your friend Theo is fine too. He's in the room next door. You're a very lucky pair of kids. What were you thinking? If you hadn't been sitting on a rubber tire, you'd probably both be dead."

"What about Latimore?" I blurt, reassembling last night's chaotic scene in my mind. "I mean—our principal. Is she okay?"

"Yes, thanks to the other boy," the doctor confirms. "If he hadn't pushed her clear of the lightning strike, she would have been electrocuted."

"Did somebody tell *her* that?" I probe. "Declan—the kid—he has kind of a reputation. The last thing he needs is to get in trouble for tackling a principal."

The doctor nods. "He's a hero. So is your other friend—the girl."

"Portia?" I ask.

"Remarkable young person. She was trained in CPR. She performed chest compressions on you and Theo. Without her, you might have both gone into heart failure."

For the first time since coming awake, I feel a tiny urge to grin tugging at the corners of my mouth. Of course Portia is trained in CPR, just like she volunteers at a food bank, and plants trees on Earth Day, and is perfect in every way. Why didn't I know that?

"As it is," the doctor goes on, "you've suffered considerable burns. I'm sure you've noticed the bandages on your arm and shoulder."

Burns! No wonder my arm hurts. "I ache in a lot of other places too. Especially my jaw."

He nods. "The body responds to a shock by tensing all muscles. They usually relax again in a few days. The burns will be a slower recovery. In your case, though, the scarring will be minimal. As I said, you and your friend Theo were *very* lucky to be on that tire."

I want to tell him that luck had nothing to do with it. It was careful planning, regardless of whether we used a bouncy castle or a rubber tire as an insulator. But then he might ask what we were planning *for*, and it's not a good idea to answer that. The fact that we knew exactly what we were doing makes it look worse, not better.

So I just say, "I guess you're right about that."

The doctor jots a few more notes on my chart and steps away from the bed. "Your mom has been in the waiting room all night and all day. I think it's time we brought her in."

My *mom*? I don't have a mom. He must mean Jenna.

But the thought causes me to conjure up a picture of my real mother—and it's the same faceless image as before.

I still can't remember her.

It didn't work. The realization is so deflating that I'm amazed I don't shrivel into something the size of a gum wrapper on the mattress. *We almost got ourselves killed and it still didn't work!*

Of course we never had any guarantee that re-creating that first lightning strike when we were in the incubator would undo the Phenomenon. There wasn't any scientific reason to believe it would work. There isn't any science in the Phenomenon to begin with.

Fact is, this was always a long shot. And like most long shots, it failed.

And then Jenna's at my bedside, hugging me, laughing and crying at the same time. It's exactly what Mom would do if she was here. And since she can't be, I'm glad I've got Jenna.

"What were you doing up there?" she sobs. "I've asked Declan again and again, and he won't give me an answer!"

Good old Declan. I kept his secrets, and now he's keeping mine.

But I have to tell Jenna something. No way are she and Willis going to believe that sheer random chance brought me to a mini-planetarium on the roof, connected to the lightning rod by coat hangers.

"It was a science experiment," I offer.

"A science experiment? Getting struck by lightning?"

"We were studying the properties of insulation," I lie. "You know, the rubber tire we were sitting on?" She's about to go ballistic on me, so I quickly add, "You don't have to tell me. Of course it was stupid. I promise I'll never do anything like that again."

"Why can't you dissect a frog like everybody else?" she demands tearfully, but she lets the subject drop. I guess when you're Declan's mother, you learn to overlook a few things that defy explanation. A promise never to do it again is the best you can hope for.

I sleep a lot after Jenna leaves, and the next time I wake up, I've got more company. Theo sits propped in a wheelchair, looking approximately how I feel. Maybe worse. Some of his hair has been singed off, including one eyebrow. His burn bandage is on the left side—the mirror image of mine, which makes sense, since we were sitting opposite each other on the tire. An IV bag dangles from the pole over his chair, matching the one that dangles over me. A sticker on the armrest declares: PROPERTY OF MEMORIAL HOSPITAL.

Memorial. We're right back where we started.

Theo breaks into a grin when he sees I'm awake. "Hey, sleeping beauty. How do you feel?"

I'm glad to see him—honest, I am. I'm thrilled that he's okay. But I can't keep my disappointment from bubbling over. "I feel like we went through all this for nothing!"

He seems surprised—doubly so because of that missing eyebrow. "For nothing?"

"It didn't work," I mourn. "I can't remember my mother and I'm stuck with your plants and karate. The Phenomenon is still going, bad as ever. We couldn't stop it—not even by burning our arms off."

"You mean you haven't noticed it yet?" Theo asks.

"Noticed what?"

"We haven't gotten our old memories back—you're right about that. But so far, there aren't any new ones. Not since the lightning strike."

I scour my mind, searching for the recollections that I've come to know as Theo's. The gardening moments. The conflicts with his dad. Karate classes and meetings with Dr. Abagnale. Close encounters with Jaws. Theo's memories just *feel* a little different because he's the person they happened to. They even look slightly different because he's a couple of inches taller than me.

My Theo memories seem familiar. I'm pretty sure I've experienced them all before. He's right! There's nothing new, and the fog of confusion that hung over everything is gone. "So what you're saying is—"

"We thought we could reverse the Phenomenon and set everything back to the way it was before. But maybe it doesn't work that way. Maybe you can stop it, but you can't undo it. That would mean last night was a total success. The Phenomenon is over. But the memories we already swapped can't be unswapped."

I think it over. It makes sense. If two kids are trading baseball cards, the cards don't automatically return to their original owners if their parents shut them down. Theo and I may have cut off the game, but the trades we made while the Phenomenon was in force are still with us, in one head or the other.

"It's good news," Theo persists. "I mean, we've got our lives back! We don't have to worry about getting lost trying to find our own homes. We can relearn our class schedules. We can study for tests without forgetting everything by exam day."

I nod soberly. He's right. No question that the Phenomenon being over is a really great thing for both of us. Our situation was desperate. That's why it called for such desperate measures. The blizzard of old memories out and new ones in was so dizzying that we couldn't function anymore. I was afraid to take a shower for fear of washing my notes off my arms and legs.

We beat a phenomenon we had no chance of understanding, much less figuring out how to stop. It's a success story. A miracle, really.

But.

"My mom," I say quietly, because this is Theo, and there are no secrets between us. If anybody understands what it's like to be me, it's him. "I forgot her. And I'm never going to get her back."

Theo taps his temple. "She's not gone. I've got her right here, and I promise I'll never forget. Anything you want to know—any one of your old memories you want me to tell you about—all you have to do is ask."

I gaze at him dubiously.

"Like Halloween when you were eight," he persists. "Your mom spent almost an hour painting a clown face on you. And before you even got out of the house, your hand got squished in the door and you cried, smearing all that makeup. So she switched your clown suit for a lab coat, spiked your hair on end, and you went trick-or-treating as a mad scientist. You got more candy that night than any other Halloween."

I can't help smiling. "Thanks, man." And I'm grateful. Really, I am. But hearing about someone isn't the same as *remembering*—seeing her in your mind, hearing her voice. And when that person is your mom, it's extra important.

Theo and I have both lost chunks of our lives, but it isn't equal—not even close. And it's never going to be.

"There you are!" Mr. Metzinger barges into my room. "I found him!" he calls into the hall. To his son, he says, "What are you doing here, Theo? You're supposed to be in bed!"

"I heard Reef was awake," Theo tells his father. "I talked one of the nurses into putting me in this wheelchair."

Mr. Metzinger flashes the two of us a broad grin. "You two guys—you slay me. I did a lot of wild things as a kid, but this was off the charts! And I was no slouch when I was your age. I used to rule the school!"

"Rule the school?" Theo looks blank. "What's that supposed to mean?"

Seriously? Theo must have heard his dad use that phrase five hundred times.

As Theo frowns in perplexity, I take stock of the memories lined up in my mind like toy soldiers.

I guess I'm not the only one who'll need help with the missing pieces going forward.

Forward. We might not have solved everything, but at least there's a way forward for us.

CHAPTER THIRTY-TWO

THEO METZINGER

Portia has a boyfriend.

No, it's not me, unfortunately. It isn't Reef either. It's this kid Nate Olberman.

Declan is disgusted with me. "You blew it, dude. All you had to do was ask. And you let yourself get stuck in the friend zone."

He's right about the friend zone, but not about the reason I got stuck there. I never asked Portia out because I knew Reef had a crush on her. And Reef knew how *I* felt about her, so he didn't make a move either. So if Declan needs to blame something, try the Phenomenon. That's what took us both out of the running and cleared a path for Hated Nate.

It's an unfair nickname because Nate Olberman is actually a pretty nice guy. But one nickname deserves another—he was the first kid to call me Basket Case in my early days coming to Delgado. Anyway, I don't mind so much that he's dating Portia and I'm not. Okay, that's a lie. But if I'd started going out with Portia, I might have lost Reef as a friend, and nothing's worth that. Once you've been inside a guy's head—and he's been inside yours—you know the meaning of close. The Phenomenon was awful, but I can't regret it because of what it created between Reef and me.

Besides, Portia and I are great friends. I try not to think of that as the consolation prize. We still volunteer together at Neighborhood Harvest—although nowadays I get a ride to Breezeway, rather than biking halfway across town in the winter. We hang out together with Reef and Declan and, yeah, even Hated Nate. We eat a ridiculous amount of fro-yo. Portia calls it burn-recovery medicine. For her, there's no such thing as a bad reason to eat fro-yo.

Reef and I had to keep the bandages on our arms and shoulders for ten days, but by then, the worst of the pain had subsided. The itch is another matter. The doctor warned us to avoid scratching in order to allow the skin to heal. Sometimes it gets so bad I want to scream.

With the bandages gone, you can't really tell I'm not a hundred percent. Well, not unless you're expecting me to have a left eyebrow. That's going to take months to come back.

"Have more fro-yo" is Portia's recommendation. "It's eyebrow-regrowth formula."

It's been three weeks since that night in the cupola, and the Phenomenon seems to be gone for good. All our forgetfulness, our confusion, our disorientation disappeared with it. It left a lot of our memories in the wrong head, but we can deal with that. At least we're ourselves again. I erased my life notes from my phone. Reef washed his arms and legs for the first time in weeks.

It's a pretty happy ending . . . except for the poor kid who can't remember his mother.

"What's a hound's tooth?" Reef asks.

"Not *a* hound's tooth," I tell him. "Houndstooth. It's the design on the skirt—kind of a small funky checkered pattern."

He frowns. "So why didn't you just say checkered?"

"You asked for details. Your mom was wearing a houndstooth skirt. The wraparound kind with a big safety pin."

"Okay, okay," Reef says quickly. "Keep going."

We're in Reef's room at the Helmer house, sitting cross-legged on the carpet. We've been having these "remembering" sessions more and more often, where one of us narrates a lost memory to the person who should own it. Reef rocks gently back and forth, his eyes squeezed shut, trying to "see" what I'm describing.

"She's got you in her arms and the two of you are going up and down as the merry-go-round turns. Pretty fast too. You can see the carnival going by, and it's mostly just a blur."

He's concentrating intently. "How old am I?"

"Little. It's not hard for her to carry you. Plus you're scared out of your wits. You haven't stopped crying the whole time. Kind of a wimp, to be honest."

"Memories only," Reef murmurs, still in the zone. "Keep your opinions to yourself. I'm having a nice moment with my mom."

"Whoops—not anymore," I inform him. "You just barfed all over the houndstooth skirt. Yuck. What was she feeding you?"

We both end up laughing. That's definitely something different about Reef. He smiles a lot more, even when he's thinking about his mother. The memories he's lost to me are out of his reach forever. But I'm still here to describe them to him, so they're never totally gone. He says that sometimes, when I give a lot of detail, he can block out all distractions and almost—*almost*—see his mom.

The day he told me that, I promised myself that I'd continue to do this for him until we're both a hundred. Memory isn't a total antidote to grief, but in a way, you can keep someone alive in your thoughts. That's what Reef says.

We'll make it work.

We have remembering sessions for me too, but mine aren't nearly as meaningful. Usually, I just end up hearing about a fishing expedition or camping trip with Dad where I failed some manhood test and got chewed out. I know that sounds bad, but to be honest, my father and I have been getting along so well lately it's almost scary. Maybe that's because Dad knows how close Reef and I came to not making it off that roof. Whatever. The point is, sometimes what you have in the present is better than anything you can dig out of the past.

"Let's do one more memory," Reef requests. "Something where I'm a little older. No puking this time."

"Got it."

There's a loud crash downstairs, followed by scrambling feet, and then Carolyn's angry shout: "Reef, get down here! Your stupid rabbit's loose again!"

Reef holds his head. "Jaws. I think he's figured out how to open his cage."

That's another new development since our stay at Memorial Hospital, Round 2. Reef has adopted Jaws as a pet. It makes sense, because Jaws adopted Reef the minute he laid his beady little eyes on him. At first it seemed like a win-win-win: I was happy to get the rabbit away from my garden; Dad was happy that the two of us had one less thing to fight about; and Jenna was happy because having an animal to take care of would "be good for the kids." The problem is that Jaws is still Houdini, regardless of whether he's in Breezeway or back in my neighborhood.

We make it downstairs just in time to see a blur of brown fur darting through the living room, with Liam and Carolyn in hot pursuit.

"Sorry!" Reef exclaims. "He's an outdoor rabbit, and he's having trouble adjusting to cage living!"

Liam, the football player, launches a pretty athletic diving tackle. Jaws squirts easily out of his reach, but Carolyn goes down like a sack of oats.

A cackle comes from Declan, who watches from the couch, his feet up on the coffee table. "Don't apologize, Reef. Adopting that little monster is the best idea you ever had!"

Jaws darts out of the living room and under the saloon doors to the kitchen. A moment later, Jenna appears. "I hope no one was counting on dinner. Jaws is in the salad spinner."

"He always did have a healthy appetite," I confess, feeling a little guilty.

At that moment, Jaws spots Reef through the glass container. Instantly, the rabbit bounds out and hops over to snuggle on his master's feet. Reef bends down and picks him up, stroking the soft brown fur. "You're okay, Jaws. Everything's fine."

"Except the salad," Declan puts in from his perch on the couch. "And Carolyn's nose."

"Shut up," she mutters, holding a paper towel to her left nostril, which is oozing pink.

The front of Reef's shirt turns suddenly dark as Jaws pees on it.

It breaks the mood. The Helmer house rocks on its foundation with laughter. Even Reef joins in, and he's the guy in the wet shirt.

Standing at the foot of the stairs, I have a sudden flashback from Reef's memory. He's at the front door with Jenna, a backpack over his shoulder.

"Let's all make Reef feel welcome," Jenna is saying to her kids. And from the resentment on their faces, I can tell she doesn't mean for the next hour or maybe a day or two. Reef has already been bunking with the Helmers while his mom is in the hospital. But something has changed—something huge.

This is the moment Reef came to stay *forever*, because he had nowhere else to go. Which means this must be the day his mother died. I can sense the weight of his grief pressing down on him. It's so dense and overpowering that I can't read his thoughts. Still, I know what they are: *This is not my home. This will never be my home.*

I look at Reef now. He *is* home.

And, sure, that might seem like an outsider's opinion, but I'm no outsider. I picture two newborn babies in that incubator when the lightning hit. That was us, closer than close.

It's still us today.

That's something to remember.

ABOUT THE AUTHOR

GORDON KORMAN wrote his first novel, *This Can't Be Happening at MacDonald Hall*, when he was thirteen years old. Since then, he's written over a hundred other books, including the #1 *New York Times* bestseller *Restart*, the Sydney Taylor Honor Book *Linked, Slacker, War Stories*, and his most recent *New York Times* bestseller, *The Fort*. He lives in Long Island with his family and can be found online at gordonkorman.com.